The Seventh Swan

BY

Bethany Maines

Blue Zephyr Press
2661 N. Pearl, #360
Tacoma WA 98407

Cover art by **LILT**.

ISBN-10: 1-7320863-9-7
ISBN-13: 978-1-7320863-9-5

Acknowledgments

Many thanks to my many beta readers who helped bring this story to life and insisted that my potted plants be space-ready and gravity accurate.

Table of Contents

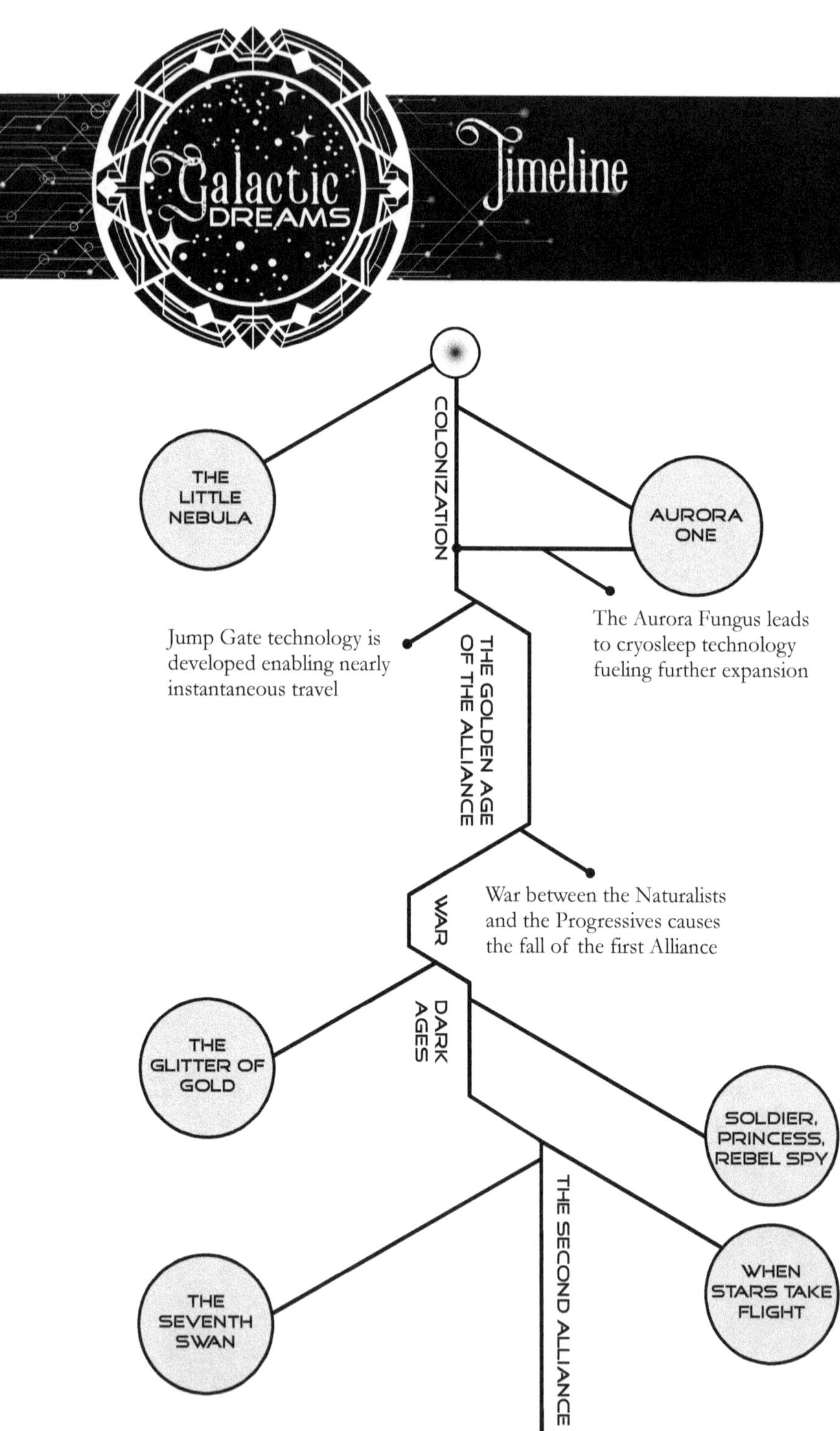

Galactic DREAMS
Timeline
COLONIZATION
THE LITTLE NEBULA
AURORA ONE
Jump Gate technology is developed enabling nearly instantaneous travel
The Aurora Fungus leads to cryosleep technology fueling further expansion
THE GOLDEN AGE OF THE ALLIANCE
War between the Naturalists and the Progressives causes the fall of the first Alliance
WAR
DARK AGES
THE GLITTER OF GOLD
SOLDIER, PRINCESS, REBEL SPY
THE SECOND ALLIANCE
THE SEVENTH SWAN
WHEN STARS TAKE FLIGHT

Introduction

WHAT IF...

...in the future the stars must fight to save humanity?
...an algae farmer's daughter and a spy make a deadly bargain to save everything they both love?
...a silent engineer on an empty moon can save a prince from an ancient evil?

Welcome to the universe of Galactic Dreams, where fairy tales are reimagined for a new age—the future. In each Galactic Dreams Volume 2 novella you'll find an old tale reborn with a mixture of romance, technology, aliens and adventure. But this time, each Prince and Princess, each band of intrepid heroes, is fighting the same enemy — an entity so vast that he can span centuries and not everyone is guaranteed to survive.

Galactic Dreams is a unique series of science-fiction novellas from Blue Zephyr Press featuring retellings of classic tales from different authors, all sharing the same universe, technology, and history.

We hope you enjoy this adventure.

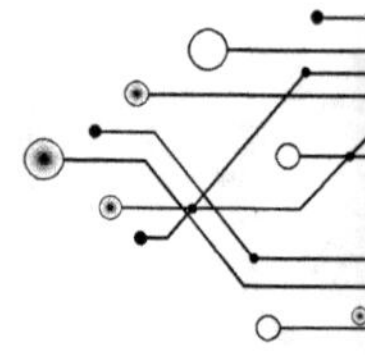

BETHANY MAINES

The boys, seeing that someone was approaching from afar, thought that their dear father was coming to them. Full of joy, they ran to meet him. Then the Queen threw one of the shirts over each of them, and when the shirts touched their bodies they were transformed into swans, and they flew away over the woods.

The Queen went home very pleased, believing that she had gotten rid of the children. However, the girl had not run out with her brothers, and the queen knew nothing about her.

Jacob and Wilhelm Grimm, The Six Swans

Chapter 1

KEELIA BLACK AND THE END OF THE BLACK LIGHT

Keelia Black of the Swan Clan watched through the domed glass of the hanger deck as her ship, the *Black Light*, exploded in a fiery blossom, beautiful and silent against the inky blackness of space. In front of her, Easton, her second oldest brother, dropped to his knees and began the Prayers for the Damned.

"You have just violated intergalactic law," said Niall, the eldest, his voice hoarse with rage.

Fang Nazari laughed. It wasn't a mad laugh. Or even particularly evil. Fang was delighted, as if Niall had promised her double desserts after dinner. "I know!" She drew a deep breath, as if inhaling the smell of victory. "And wasn't it fun!"

Keelia turned and examined their captor more closely. Fang was nearly eight feet tall—either space-born or modified—and she didn't walk so much as glide. Or perhaps it was her dress that moved? The fabric, if it could be called that, moved around Fang as if made of millions of tiny green iridescent insects. Occasionally, bits of her dress broke away from the mass and crawled up into her turquoise hair and sometimes into her mouth, where she ate them with an audible crunch.

Keelia and her six brothers, Niall, the twins Easton and Graves, Jedidiah, Anwell, and Mataxlen had arrived in the quadrant earlier in the week. Alliance surveys had indicated that it was uninhabited, but likely to hold profitable asteroids. The Black children had harvested two ice rocks and were looking for dwarf star alloy when their scans picked up an asteroid the size of a small moon with multiple alloy pings. They had landed, prepared to do a survey and a little exploratory digging with their father's newest invention—a sonic drill.

What they had found was a moon base, a mad woman, an army of robots and what appeared to be a seven-foot man-alligator. Fang Nazari, as she had introduced herself, had wasted no time in launching one of her robots armed with a detonator and a cubic meter of the highly explosive dwarf star alloy at their ship.

And now their ship, and their way home, was dust and debris.

The circular hanger was a donut shape. At the center was a shaft dug into the side of the asteroid—meant for venting engine exhaust into space. A force field kept the atmosphere in the hanger deck and out of the shaft, allowing them all to breathe. Deep below them, Keelia could see that the turbines and gravshields were inert, meaning the shaft wasn't in use at the moment. She couldn't imagine what kind of engine would require a vent shaft that big. Above them, inside the shaft and exposed to space, a complex arrangement of scaffolding, handles and cables proliferated, allowing only glimpses of the dark expanse of space beyond.

Around them stood a cadre of robots, led by the commands and tail flicks of the alligator-looking creature that was almost as tall as Fang. He snarled at every move the Blacks made, but once their mistress had called a halt, neither he or the robots had moved.

Behind Fang stood three humans, none of whom had taken part in the fighting. The first was a man with dark-fringed eyes, a thick beard, and long black hair tied up in a knot on his head. He held his hands in front of him as if they were in chains, although no cuffs were in evidence. The second was a woman with broad shoulders and green hair. The third, an older man, had short white hair, red-rimmed eyes, and gnarled hands. All three of them were filthy with dark dust and watched the Black children with flat, impassive expressions, as if they had seen this show before.

"Your actions indicate that you would like war with the Alliance," said Niall. It was a stall. Everyone knew that this far out, the law of the Alliance wasn't worth the data stream it was imprinted on. It was really just to give Easton time to make contact. Every morning the telepaths on each ship of the Swan Clan received an image of who the Swan Emergency Beacon would be that day. Today it had been their mother, her hair, red like Keelia's own, vibrant in the rendering. Easton was attempting to calm his mind and send a distress call. They all knew what the odds were. Their mother was a very long way away and no one could possibly reach them for months. But, at the very least, the Swan Clan would descend in fiery retribution. That seemed like cold comfort at the moment.

"The Alliance doesn't exist here," snapped Fang. "There is only me or space. So now you have a choice. If you'll notice, there are escape pods around the room."

"Mat," said Niall, pointing at their youngest brother. Mataxlen jogged to the nearest pod, jostling past the cylindrical robots who creaked in protest.

"The pods are standard issue: enough fuel for a short directional thruster burst, twenty-four hours of air, and only short-range communications," said Fang pleasantly. "Or so I'm told."

"Air and fuel tanks look full," said Mat, running back. "She's not lying. Also, Dura-flex coating and a docking arm." There was an exchange of looks. Dura-flex coating was resilient, flexible and could withstand the outer corona of a sun, such as the one located a short distance from their position. A docking arm meant that the pods could be linked. Their possibilities for escape had just expanded.

Easton chanted softly, leaning against his twin's leg for stability.

"You got here in a very lovely, very large ship with a lot of air and fuel. I'm sure you know exactly how far those pods will take you," said Fang, smiling gleefully, unaware of the subtle shift of mood in the Blacks. "I'm sure you will acknowledge that the pods are simply a prolonged method of suicide. But I do have another option for you."

"What's that?" asked Niall.

"Work for me," said Fang, crunching a piece of her dress between her teeth. "I'm in need of experienced diggers."

"Pods," said Niall, without hesitation.

Fang looked mildly surprised. "Interesting choice. You did hear me state twenty-four hours of air, right?"

"Pods," said Niall again.

"Before you commit, I feel I should point out a few little… problems with the pods."

"Such as?" Niall's face had hardened into angular planes, his jaw clenched so hard that Keelia was worried for his teeth. Of all of them, he looked like a true Swan—thick, white-blonde hair, light brown skin, aquiline nose and a square jaw. Her brothers were all variations on the theme—some more brunette than others, but all with the same blue eyes. She was the one who stood out, with her mother's fiery red hair and her father's green eyes.

"Well, for instance, there is no internal release. In order to eject, someone has to manually release each escape pod. And of course, there is the fact that the release buttons are all inside the exhaust shaft." She pointed upward.

"You mean, someone has to stay behind," said Niall.

"Is that what it means?" asked Fang with a wicked grin. "I should also point out that whoever stays behind would have to use this air canister and it only has three minutes of air." She patted a breather mask and canister next to her.

"Our suit tanks all had more air," said Niall pointing to the collection of canisters that had been ripped from their suits along with their helmets when they had surrendered.

"What tanks?" asked Fang, and the droids promptly began to crush the tanks in pinching claws, the tubes popping and leaking the air out in angry gusts.

"Right," said Niall.

"The other problem," continued Fang, "is that the computer estimates that it would take someone five minutes," she traced an arc from right to left in the air, "to make it around the entire circle. Five-minute trip. Three minutes of air. You might want to factor that into your decision making."

Keelia looked up at the path that Fang had traced. It made sense that the computer would estimate that route—it was the safest. But safest also meant slowest. She could do it faster. But how much faster? Within three minutes?

Niall turned his back to Fang and surveyed his siblings. Keelia did the same. They were all fighters. Even Jed, who was their medic, was a better fighter than Keelia was. They all had more skills in piloting, flying and ship maintenance than she did. She did have one thing that they didn't—a childish talent based on stubbornness.

"Easton?" Niall asked.

Easton abruptly stopped chanting and stood up. "Mother says: *Quicquid capit.*"

They all nodded—they knew the family motto.

"Who stays?" asked Niall.

"That's me," said Keelia.

"Can't be you," said Anwell. "Everyone knows Dad wants to leave you the business." It was a family joke. Everyone knew Dad didn't have a business. He had a lab, mad dreams and crazy inventions that Mom turned into a business. Langston Black invented things. Rayna Black kept them all flying. Keelia had been the first in the family to go to an official school. She was only working with her brothers until the Engineering Guild reviewed her test scores and approved her license.

"I'll be faster," said Anwell. "I'll do it."

Keelia shook her head. "Yes, you and Niall are faster than me in low grav, but I can hold my breath the longest," said Keelia. "The best shot for everyone is if I do it."

They all looked to Niall. She didn't have to add that she would be counting on them to come back for her. That was a given.

Niall reluctantly nodded once and then all nodded together and began to move, running for their pods.

Niall hugged her tightly, for only a second.

"You stay alive," he whispered in her ear. "Whatever it takes."

Quicquid capit.

Then he was gone.

Keelia turned back to Fang who was watching open mouthed as the brothers dispersed. Behind her she heard the sound of running feet and the first pod slam shut.

"You must be just the biggest wet blanket at crew parties," said Fang, staring down at Keelia as if she were a new and disgusting form of mold.

Keelia steadied herself, trying not to feel the loss of her wall of brothers as she stared up at the pale face of Fang Nazari, with her red slash of a mouth and deep black eyes. Keelia didn't answer Fang. Her voice would probably shake anyway and she didn't want to embarrass the family. Fang would never know that she was scared, that her mouth was dry and her palms were wet inside her space suit. She marched past the towering woman and picked up the breather apparatus, weighing it in her hands.

Fang slid around in front of her, watching her with eager eyes. As if genuinely interested to see what Keelia would do next.

"Three minutes of air?" Keelia asked, looking up at the levers and buttons.

"Three minutes," said Fang reassuringly. Behind her, the man with the long black hair shook his head in a small negative gesture and held up two fingers.

"Good to know," said Keelia, and strapped on the face mask.

Niall was stepping into his pod. Keelia tightened down the straps on the mask, started her watch and hit the oxygen apparatus to start the flow. Then she sprinted across the access ramp to the exhaust shaft and launched herself upward into space.

Chapter 2

JERICHO NAZARI AND WHAT HAPPENED NEXT

Jericho Nazari watched his step-mother grimace in anger as the girl jumped. Fang had never been prepared for others to have original thoughts. She disliked it intensely. She preferred all thinking to originate with her.

The others he'd seen try this had all jumped out and up, intending to sail through the gravity-free space to the far-right lever. It was a safe route, but slow. No one ever went left. Left was a tangle of live plasma cables. The girl did neither—she launched herself straight up, caught the platform above her head and pulled herself onto the top of it. Now above the layer of cables, she flung herself at the left-most pod. Back-flipping as she went, she hit the platform feet first, locked in with her suit's magnetic boots to keep from sliding off and slammed the button down. Jericho checked the clock: fifteen seconds, one pod away.

The crew of the *Black Light* had fought and acted with the discipline and efficiency he expected from a military unit. They wasted no time and obeyed every order from their leader. It was the kind of obedience that was only offered to someone that had earned complete trust. So when the Captain had embraced the girl, Jericho had fully expected the man to stay—that it had been a farewell between lovers. Instead, the girl was left behind.

She was now pulling herself hand over hand along the plasma cables to the second lever. Her gloves were smoking. They would not be safe for space after this. She locked her boots into the armature surrounding the lever, reached up and slammed the button. Thirty seconds, second pod away.

She pushed off across the space toward the third station.

Even if she hadn't been the only woman on the crew, she would have been remarkable. Her hair was long—unusual for a space faring people who preferred to keep hair short and out of helmet seals. Hers swung in two thick rope-like braids around her waist. And the color... Copper, orange, blonde and red all mixed and flickered as she moved, like a flame.

She landed at the third station and released the next pod.

She had to be burning through the oxygen, but at this rate it didn't matter. She would have them all away by the time the tank exhausted itself. The next station would be the true test. The gap between three and four was long, and she would have to make a long slow sail across the open shaft.

Once again, the girl proved that *have to* wasn't in her vocabulary. She threw herself feet first at the force field wall between the exhaust shaft and the hanger bay. But instead of bouncing off the shimmering wall of energy, she began to run along it, her boots sparking with each strike.

"How is she doing that?" snarled Fang.

Jericho had seen the trick before, just not done this elegantly. He could have told Fang that the girl had activated the magnetic lock on her boots and the weak pull from the metal beyond the field was just enough to keep her from bouncing off. Prolonged use would burn out the boot circuitry, but she wasn't holding anything back. And he wasn't about to tell his step-mother anything.

Angrily, Fang stormed to a control panel. Seconds later,

Jericho's heart dropped as he heard the exhaust turbines begin to turn over. The girl jumped out into space as the first pulse of air blasted up the shaft. The air pushed her out and away from the release button. She snagged some of the cables, gloves smoking again. She had to be feeling the heat. Precious seconds ticked by as the girl hauled herself back to the fourth button and slammed it down.

Jericho checked the outside scanners just visible to him on the far control panel. The released pods were using their docking arms to link together. This crew was sticking together no matter what.

Above him, the girl had made it to the fifth station. As the pod dropped, he checked the clock. The turbine had slowed her down. She was at one minute fifty seconds and she had to be out of air. She was moving more slowly now, angling against the wind. Was she seeing the black and white spots in her vision as her oxygen ran out? Had panic set in yet?

She jumped wide and for a moment he thought she'd massively misjudged and then another gust of air from the turbine hit and it pushed her back into the last station.

Jericho glanced at the last pod. Through the window he could see the Captain of the *Black Light* watching the girl's progress. His expression one of tense pride. Above them, the girl pounded the button down.

Nothing happened.

She hit it again, her arms flailing.

The pod dropped halfway and then the doors closed again, crushing the pod at the Captain's shoulder level. The dura-flex hull held integrity, but inside Jericho could see the Captain pinned in place and yelling in pain.

The girl hit the button again, but he could tell that she had lost strength. Fang cackled happily and turned off the turbines. Jericho watched in horror as the girl unlocked her boots. With the turbines freshly turned off there would be negative pressure, a weak atmosphere and gravity. Not locked to the armature, the girl would fall.

She inverted, and clicked the magnets on. The boots slammed her into the button. The pod dropped. Then her boots failed. The girl fell toward the turbines, clearly unconscious.

Jericho leapt forward and slammed his hand down on the control for the shaft net, activating the system of fine filaments and force fields that kept debris from falling into the turbines.

"You promised me more hands for the work crew," said Jericho as Fang began to lift her hand to make him stop. "You kill her, and I won't even get one."

"You're being dramatic," said Fang with a sniff. "It's not like I'm going to let the rest of them escape. Where are they going to go? All I have to do is wait until their oxygen starts to run out and then I'm sure they'll be more than happy to reconsider my offer."

"Credits in the hand are worth more than credits in the future," said Jericho, setting the shaft net to rise.

"You're always so weak," said Fang. "You know you can't save them. You can't save anyone."

Jericho gritted his teeth and ignored her, watching the progress of the net. Adjusting the atmosphere controls to block off the shaft at their level—extending the atmosphere outward.

Fang was right, of course. He couldn't save anyone. He couldn't even save himself. But maybe, for today, he could save this girl.

Fang slithered closer, her dress wrapping itself around his leg. "You're just prolonging the inevitable," she whispered. He could feel the nanites under his skin crawl as they recognized the touch of their older, bigger cousins. It made him want to rip his own skin off. The net was nearly to their level. He could see the girl sprawled out at an awkward angle, a black form against the glowing white net.

"Do you want us to dig faster or not?" he asked, turning to Fang. "More hands equals faster. It's up to you."

"It's always up to me," hissed Fang. "Don't ever forget that."

"I never do," he replied with a patience born of five and a half long years of imprisonment.

"Fine. Go get her. But if she doesn't turn out to be productive, I'll let Kodor break her neck."

Kodor grinned, showing his rows of sharp teeth, and smacked his tail on the ground. "Breakfast snacks," he said.

The number of ways in which Jericho had imagined killing Kodor was probably in the thousands. This morning, Jericho imagined beating him to death with the wrench that was only a few feet away. Jericho didn't reach for it. He knew better by now. Instead, he went past the gangly reptile and out onto the net. Walking carefully on the bouncing filament, he crossed to where the girl lay.

The filaments were meant for small space debris. The two of them together in one place might overload the net and cause it to snap. As he got closer, he lay down to distribute the weight and crawled to her. He pulled her mask off and checked her pulse. She was breathing, but it seemed shallow. He could see her palms through her gloves—they were raw, red and blistered. He looped one hand under her shoulder, hoped she didn't have any neck injuries, and began to drag her back. They were almost to the platform when he heard Fang howling. He looked up and saw her hitting Kodor.

Jericho sat on the platform while pulling the girl to him and then looked around to see what was upsetting his step-mother.

"What do you mean they're out of docking-clamp range?" she demanded, hitting Kodor again.

"They use thrusters," said Kodor, ducking and dodging the blows that rained down on him.

Jericho looked up at the screen. The six pods had linked themselves together and then burned all of the thrusters from one pod to maneuver the entire unit into the orbit of the nearby star. He realized suddenly what their plan was. But what would it get them? Twenty-four hours in a pod? Did they have another ship?

"What are they doing?" howled Fang, smacking at the controls. "Launch the robots! Get them back here!"

"The robots can't take the heat from the star," said Kodor. "They will melt."

"Launch them anyway," shrieked Fang.

Kodor nodded, but Jericho noticed that he was only selecting the oldest and smallest of the army to launch. The ones that were already more likely to malfunction.

Jericho hefted the girl over his shoulder and jerked his head at Sadiki and Phaedra, heading for the lift. He didn't want to be around when Fang realized that her prey had escaped.

"I don't understand," said Phaedra as the lift door closed. "What were they doing?" She looked from Sadiki to Jericho for an explanation.

"Using the thrusters of the pods in unison, they might be able to time the gravity and orbit of the star to sling-shot themselves out of the quadrant," said Jericho. "But anything less than all six pods and they wouldn't have the mass to make it work."

Phaedra looked at the girl over Jericho's shoulder. "So she had to get all six pods free or none of them escaped." Jericho nodded. "Do you think they'll do it?" she asked, looking at the ceiling as if she could see through the rock and metal to the stars above.

"I think a crew that goes from captured to escaping in under five minutes is not going to miss their burn window," said Jericho.

"Yeah, but they had to leave her to do it. How do you make that decision?" asked Phaedra.

"Maybe they thought her chances of survival were better if she stayed," offered Sadiki. He rarely spoke these days and his voice was gravelly with disuse. "There's only twenty-four hours of oxygen in those pods and no cryosleep options. How far can they get?"

"I don't know," said Jericho. "Maybe far enough."

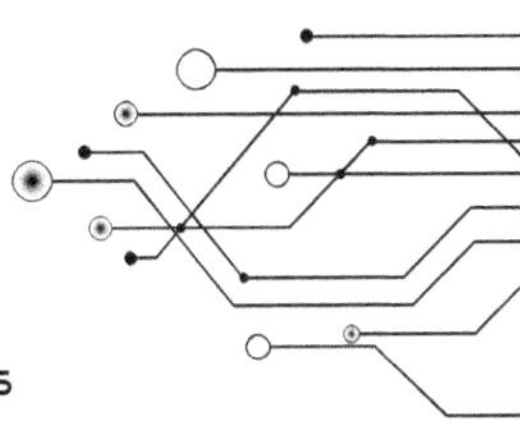

Chapter 3

NIALL AND THE BLACK SWAN BROTHERS

Niall was fairly certain that a piece of the pod was sticking into his shoulder. But the lights had gone out in his pod and he couldn't see anything. He fumbled his left hand at the controls, unable to move his right. He finally found the communications diode and hailed his brothers.

"Status?" he croaked.

"Moving toward the star," said Graves. "Out of reach of their docking clamp. I expect they'll be firing robots soon. Mat hopes to have us in the corona shortly. What's your status?"

"Injured," said Niall. "Right arm unmovable."

"Can you still reach your emergency kit?" asked Graves.

Niall checked. Reaching to his right side with his left arm proved to be a torture of screaming pain. "I'll make it happen," he said when he had recovered his breath. "What does Easton say of Keelia?"

"Unconscious," said Graves. "But alive."

Niall let out his breath and clunked his head back against the padding.

"She was amazing," said Mat, his voice hardly more than a whisper on the coms.

"No wonder she always kicked my ass at ship tag," said Anwell. There was a long moment of silence over the coms and they all watched the star draw closer.

"Burn in twenty minutes thirty seconds," said Mat. Niall tried to set his watch and realized he couldn't.

"Matty, you'll have to mark me," said Niall. "I'm flying blind over here."

"Will do," replied Mat. He was their pilot and there was no one Niall would rather have setting their course.

"What if they kill her?" asked Jed, the family medic.

"Then we will burn them all and blow that *fjandinn* asteroid into dust," said Niall.

"Can we do that anyway?" asked Anwell.

Niall felt blood trickling out of the wound in his shoulder. "I kind of think we should," he said.

"Niall?" asked Graves, his voice worried. Easton was the telepath and Graves was the empath. Between the two of them, nothing much happened aboard the *Black Light* without them knowing about it. And when Easton went into one of his trances, his twin was the only one he would communicate with.

"I'm all right," said Niall. "I'll make it."

"Graves, how bad is he? Is he going to make it through the transition?" That was Jed, worrying about the next step of their plan.

"I said I'll make it," said Niall. "Just concentrate on helping Mat get us out of here."

"Incoming," said Anwell, whose pod was facing backward toward the asteroid. Then he laughed. "Never mind. They're melting."

Niall heard the *ping, ping* of metal droplets hitting the outside of his pod as the robots melted down in the heat of the star.

There was silence over the coms and Niall tried to find that reassuring. His brothers knew better than to waste battery power with idle chatter. But instead he felt isolated and worried. He wondered how much worse it was going to be for Keelia when she woke up without them. He was the big brother. He was supposed to keep her safe. On the other hand, she really could hold her breath longer. If it had been him out there, then it was entirely possible that not all of them would have made it. And if she'd been in this pod, the crush point would have occurred at her head height. Logically, he'd made the right decision.

"Burn coming up on my mark," said Matty. Mat, Niall self-corrected. Mat and Keelia were really too old to be going by childhood nicknames. But in his heart, they were still chubby toddlers, and he felt afraid for his tiny sister.

"Three, two, and… mark."

Niall hit the thrusters and he felt his pod jerk forward as the others did too. Unexpectedly, he also began to feel the heat from the star, even through the shielding. This was not going to be a comfortable ride.

He was right.

The pods were not intended for that speed of travel, and between the heat and the gravitational forces pulling at his wound, he was in screaming agony for the duration. He was delirious and drenched when the pods finally slowed. He couldn't tell if it was blood, sweat, or puke, but it didn't matter. They had succeeded.

"Niall!" That was Graves, yelling at him. He wondered how long Graves had been yelling.

"I'm here," said Niall flipping the com on. "Did everyone make it?"

"We're all here," responded Graves.

"Good. Proceed to Emergency Plan Zed. Sound check upon activation."

"Easton's already in," said Graves.

"Activating now," said Mat.

"Activating now," said Anwell.

"Activating now," said Jed.

"That's not what they mean," said Graves.

"I know what they mean," said Niall, struggling to reach for his emergency pack. He finally located the single injection spray. The one that no one was supposed to ever have to use. He injected directly into his neck and immediately felt the cold numbness of the Aurora Fungus spread outwards, along his limbs. The space-born, oxygen devouring, cell-freezing fungus was the originator of all cryosleep technology and was theoretically a banned substance. But the Swan Clan had been breeding it for the last twenty years—it was one of their secrets. It was unstable and potentially deadly—the success rate for bringing someone back was about seventy-five percent—but if the choice was death or freezing, they all knew what to do. *Quicquid capit.* Whatever it takes to survive.

"Activating now," he said. "I love you all too. I swear, we'll get her back."

He didn't doubt that the family would come. They always did. And when they did, he was going to kill Fang Nazari.

The sun was about to go down when she heard a rushing sound and saw six swans fly in through the window. Landing on the floor, they blew on one another, and blew all their feathers off. Then their swan-skins came off, just like shirts. The girl looked at them and recognized her brothers. She was happy and crawled out from beneath the bed. The brothers were no less happy to see their little sister, but their happiness did not last long.

"You cannot stay here," they said to her. "This is a robbers' den. If they come home and find you, they will murder you."

"Can't you protect me?" asked the little sister.

"No," they answered. "We can take off our swan-skins for only a quarter hour each evening. Only during that time do we have our human forms. After that we are again transformed into swans."

Crying, the little sister said, "Can you not be redeemed?"

"Alas, no," they answered. "The conditions are too difficult. You would not be allowed to speak or to laugh for six years, and in that time you would have to sew together six little shirts from asters for us. And if a single word were to come from your mouth, all your work would be lost."

Jacob and Wilhelm Grimm, The Six Swans

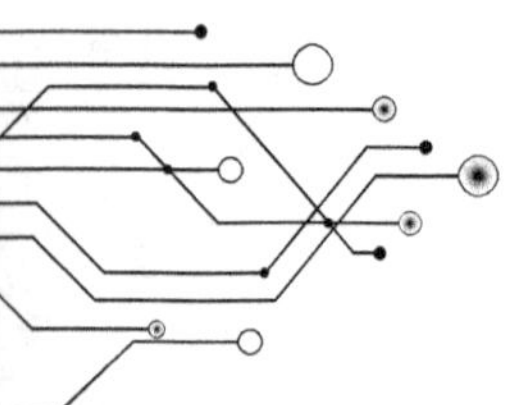

Chapter 4

KEELIA LANDS IN THE FRYING PAN

Keelia knew she was awake because she was in pain. Her left shoulder was in agony, her hands were completely numb, and she couldn't see. She thrashed and realized she was in restraints.

"Please refrain from moving," said a soothing, automated voice. "Medical procedures are ongoing."

"Where am I?" whispered Keelia.

"You are in Medical Tube Number Three. You have sustained burns, a dislocated shoulder and subconjunctival hemorrhaging."

Keelia tried to focus on something that wasn't her list of injuries. What would be most helpful to her? "Where is Med-Tube number three located?"

"In the medical bay."

"Where is the medical bay?"

"The medical bay is on Nazari Mining Base on asteroid Seven X Twelve," said the voice.

"What are the coordinates of asteroid Seven X Twelve?"

"That information is unavailable to the medical database."

Keelia took a deep breath, feeling slightly calmer. Seven X Twelve didn't mean anything to her, but having a name made her feel more in control.

"Why can't I see?" she asked.

"We have sealed your eyes shut while we repair the hemorrhaging."

That was too much exposure to space—breather masks

weren't enough protection for what she'd done. The hands were probably from the plasma cords. She'd known she'd pay for that later. But the dislocated shoulder? She didn't remember that.

"How did I dislocate my shoulder?" she asked.

"We do not have data on that," said the voice. "Evidence suggests an impact from a fall."

The last thing she remembered was pounding on the button for Niall's pod and seeing it stuck halfway out. She didn't even remember if she had succeeded. But if she had fallen from there, she should be dead. There hadn't been any safety nets in the exhaust shaft. Unless someone had activated it after she'd gone in? That didn't seem like something Fang Nazari would have done.

There was a pressure along her eyelids.

"You may open your eyes now," said the robotic voice.

Keelia blinked at the blue lights of the med-tube. She was wearing a long, papery-plastic medical gown that wrapped around her like a bath towel and fastened in two straps at the shoulders. There was no sign of her space suit or the clothes she'd been wearing underneath it. A robotic arm extended with a needle and plunged into her shoulder. Keelia winced and then stopped as a numbness spread outward.

"Your shoulder has been relocated to correct positioning, but you will experience some discomfort due to the injury for the next few days. Please return to the medical bay for appropriate pain medication as necessary."

"Sure," said Keelia. She wasn't sure what happened while she was unconscious, but somehow doubted that she would be allowed to pop back into the med-bay *as necessary*.

"Your treatment is complete," said the voice. "Have a nice day."

The bed she was on ejected out of the tube, and she blinked blurry-eyed at a bright room, unable to focus. She lifted a hand to block the light and a figure moved a few feet away. She tried not to panic or show fear, but she blinked more rapidly, trying to bring the room into focus.

There was the sound of a door opening and the figure stopped moving.

"You're not needed here, Kodor," said the person near her. It was a man. His voice was pleasantly deep, but his tone was angry.

"I'm here for the female," replied a voice, guttural and lisping, as if it was making words with a jaw not designed for Basic. Whoever Kodor was, he didn't sound pleasant.

"No," said the man above her. Her eyesight was improving. She could now see his general outline. "She's going back to the cell block and then she'll go into rotation when she can work."

"I'm to take her," said the first voice.

"No," said the man, and for a moment there was a soft pressure of his hand on her shoulder. She saw the shape of him move around the foot of the bed.

"Mistress says," hissed the first voice.

The room swam a little as she tried to focus, but this time she was able to make sense of the shapes. The medical bay contained at least fifteen patient areas, but the lights were only on in her pod. There were no doctors, nurses, or other patients. She was the only one. Near the door, the alligator-thing was looming over the dark-haired man who had warned her about the oxygen. He had cleaned himself up a bit, and she could see that under the grime he might be good looking, if he'd shave the beard. His sleeves were pushed up, and he had a tattoo around one forearm, high up near the elbow, of a patterned blue band about an inch thick.

"No," the man reiterated.

"Mistress give me proxy," said Kodor, lifting an elaborate filigree piece of metal.

"I don't care," said the man.

"Maybe I don't use it on you," said Kodor. "Maybe I send the bots to go find Sadiki. Bring him here."

That stopped the man. She could see hatred for the reptile etched in every line of his face.

Keelia struggled to sit up, even as the world swayed around her.

The man turned to assist her, but Kodor held the piece of metal up to his mouth. "Stop." The man grimaced, but did as he was told. "Female comes with me," said Kodor, stepping forward and grabbing her by the arm. He pulled her off the table and toward the door.

She stumbled and looked back as they exited the med-bay. The man was still standing where they had left him. He was focused on Kodor and his expression was one of black murder.

Kodor pulled her through dusty, empty halls, trailed by a contingent of the rolling cylindrical robots. The metal floor was cold under her bare feet. They entered a wide lift clearly meant for freight and rode it upward. Then it was through more corridors until they reached a maintenance bay full of dusty equipment. Each piece of equipment was labeled with the logo for the Nazari

Corporation. There was a light on at the far side of the bay and Kodor led them in that direction.

Winding their way through the equipment, they eventually came out into a wide space directly in front of two wide airlock doors. The trail of dust at the base of the doors indicated that they probably opened to the asteroid's surface. Directly under light was the thing that she and her brothers had abandoned entirely when they had been attacked—her father's latest innovation: a sonic drill.

Langston Black had no formal education, but his inventions had brought profit to all of the Swan Clan. His machines were always faster, easier to use, and burned less fuel. With his help, the Swan Clan had come to dominate the business of water reclamation and asteroid mining in three quadrants. This drill was in beta test—with a direct uplink to his lab AI. Langston had specifically asked Keelia and her brothers to take it with them, but he'd taken the usual precautions, with start-up and operation coded to the Black genetic fingerprint. If she could turn on the drill, the telemetry would be sent directly back to her father. Her family would know where to find her. Keelia felt a little blossom of hope.

Fang Nazari was circling the drill, fingering each piece as she went. She stopped briefly next to Kodor and held out her hand. Reluctantly, Kodor handed over the piece of metal he'd used to control the man in the med-bay. She snapped it back onto her ring and turned to Keelia.

"It is a drill, yes?" Fang asked, her dress sweeping her up high above Keelia.

"Yes," said Keelia, trying not to sound afraid.

"But no drill bits. This part, this uses sound waves. We have a sample tray here." She turned to Keelia, her hands clasping and un-clasping in front of her. "It uses harmonic resonance to tear a substance apart at a molecular level, doesn't it?" Fang's dress lowered her down to Keelia's level in a smooth, inhuman arc. "Tell me it does."

"Yes," said Keelia, feeling a deep seed of fear.

"Turn it on," commanded Fang. "I need to see how it works."

"Why? It's just for rock."

"When I'm done with it, it will be for so much more," whispered Fang, turning to the drill and caressing the metal skin. "I need to see how it's made. Not just the mechanics, I need the brain."

"It's just a drill," said Keelia. She was having second thoughts about turning on the drill.

"It's a weapon," said Fang. "And I need to know its every desire. I need to know the dreams it dreams." She slithered close to Keelia, her eyes burning. "I need to know its base code."

Keelia swallowed hard. If Fang cracked the shell of the drill, she would have access to the link the drill shared with her father's lab computer. That computer held every innovation that had driven the Swan Clan's success for the last forty years. This was no longer about Keelia's safety. This was about her family and her clan.

"No," said Keelia.

"Yes," said Fang, cheerfully.

"No," said Keelia.

"The Board expects results. You will turn it on."

"What Board?" Keelia felt lost.

"The Nazari Corporation. They think they can yank my chain just because Marid isn't here anymore." Her face reflected a bitter annoyance.

Keelia felt only slightly less lost. Who was Marid? If Fang was a Nazari, how could the Board of the company control her?

"But I'm not their dog," hissed Fang, focusing on Keelia. "They are mine. They will take this bone and they will go away. And when the time comes…" Fang stared off into space, her face registering a warm hatred and glee. "I will put them down like the animals they are." She blinked and seemed to register Keelia's presence again. "You will tell me how to turn on the machine."

"It's proprietary code. You can't access it. It belongs to the Blacks."

"Well, it belongs to me now," said Fang, moving closer. "You belong to me now. And you will turn it on for me or I will hurt you."

"You can't have it," said Keelia, fighting the urge to back away from Fang. There was a crackle of static electricity coming off the dress and she felt the hairs on her arms stand up as Fang, her faced suffused with rage, slithered within inches.

"You don't think I can handle it? You think I couldn't figure it out? You small minded little *tik*!" She slapped Keelia. "You have no idea who you're dealing with!" She struck out at Keelia again, but Keelia jerked back and the slap struck her in the throat.

Keelia staggered back clutching her throat. The blow hadn't been that strong, but it had come with a biting sting, as if the mad-woman in front of her had pricked her with something sharp.

"Tell me how to start it," commanded Fang.

"No," said Keelia. There was an immediate burning in her throat and it felt like thousands of fire ants were crawling under her skin.

"Tell me!" screamed Fang, her fists clenched in rage.

"No," said Keelia again. The pain redoubled and she dropped to her knees. "It doesn't belong to you."

Fang's dress wrapped itself around Keelia and hoisted her up to face level with Fang.

"Tell me what I want to hear, or I'll let Kodor eat you."

Keelia was finding it hard to breathe. She wasn't sure if she could beat Kodor, but she'd take her chances before she told Fang anything.

"*Bíttu mig*," said Keelia. Which was childish, but it was all she could think of.

The dress shook her back and forth like a rag doll. "You will say what I want or you won't say anything at all," hissed Fang.

Keelia had a response for that was even more childish, as well as being short, pithy and foul-mouthed, but she opened her mouth to speak and found that she could not.

Fang giggled and the dress dropped Keelia on the floor. "It's fine," said Fang, turning back to the drill. "It's fine. I can figure it out myself. It's just a drill. I'll have it figured out in no time. Like that." She snapped her fingers.

Keelia tried to yell at her, but again found that she could not. Kodor snickered at her and Keelia staggered to her feet. She wasn't sure what to do next.

"Put her with the others," said Fang, waving a hand at Kodor. "We might as well get some use out of her."

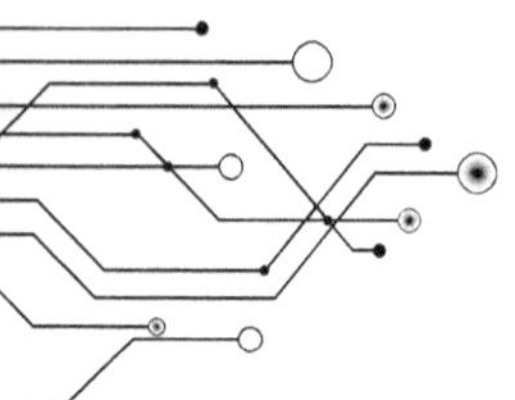

Chapter 5

JERICHO AND THE PRISONERS

Jericho tried to follow Kodor, but somewhere, Fang had commanded him to stay away. The command wasn't terribly strong—he could disobey if he really wanted to. He considered it and then chose not to. He had already pushed his luck today. He wasn't sure how much he could risk. He wanted to help the girl, but the truth was that he couldn't risk that much for a complete stranger. He felt a stab of guilt over his decision and he pushed it down. It wasn't the first time he'd had to make such a choice. It probably wouldn't be the last.

He went to find Bruges and Pavel in the Engine Room. He tapped the panel to open the door and found himself staring at the Nazari Corporation logo emblazoned on the door. He thought he'd learned to not see them, to ignore the fact that it was his name on every wall, door and piece of equipment. But today, Jericho found the Nazari logos catching his eye and it burned like the nanites under his skin, reminding him that his father was dead, and that Fang had taken what should have belonged to him.

After Marid's death, the Board of Directors had stepped in to run the business, leaving Fang and Jericho to look after the family holdings. Not that Fang cared for anything but the moon base. Jericho had inherited his father's seat on the Board, and Fang still nominally held the position of Head of Research, but Jericho thought of those positions as illusory. The only things that were real were the cold walls of the base, the hard rock of the asteroid and his four fellow prisoners.

Angrily, he slapped the door panel again and the door opened with a grinding jerk. Once inside, he found the Octoparian Bruges under water in the pumping system, his tentacles working a wrench and a pipe. Pavel clung to one of the pipes above him, welding a new section of pipe into place.

Pavel pushed up his goggles and dropped down as Jericho approached. Tall and gangly from being born in space, Pavel looked like the typical belter kid, although his buzz cut had grown out.

"Phaedra said we had seven, but ended up with one? I bet the Queen Bitch is pissed about that."

"We may not even get one," said Jericho bitterly. "I barely got her out of the med-tube when Kodor took her."

There was the sound of cursing from the pump tank and then Bruges climbed out. "Parts needed," said Bruges.

"It's not just the pumping system," said Pavel. "Cooling is about to go tits up, and fuel transfer is one *hani-upp* away from kerflooey. I don't know what's causing the degradation, but you've got to get her to put in to port somewhere." Like most residents of the Gora Eight asteroid belt, Pavel couldn't go six words without swearing.

"You don't think I'm trying?" demanded Jericho. "I have to wait until sane rolls around on her spinner, and I pushed her a bunch just to get the girl."

"You got us a girl?" Pavel perked up and Bruges hit him in the head with one of his tentacles.

"What?" demanded Pavel. "I mean, I love Phaedra, but she

doesn't swing my direction. It would be nice to have someone cuter than you two around."

"It would be nice if we didn't have to be around here at all," said Jericho.

"Well, that goes without saying," said Pavel. "But unless the Mighty Bitchtress gets us to an outpost with parts soon, none of us will be going anywhere—including her."

"I'll work on it tomorrow," said Jericho, tugging at his hair. "Do you want me to take a look at the cooling system?"

"Yes," said Bruges. "Need more arms." Jericho tried not to point out that eight would seem to be more than enough. Bruges wouldn't get the joke.

Two hours later, they were finishing up the repair when they all felt the tug under their skins that indicated that lock-down was imminent. They walked back to the cell block and Jericho scrubbed at his skin trying to rub the pipe gunk off. The amount of money he'd pay for a decent bath with actual soap increased daily. Phaedra and Sadiki met them at the entrance to their cell block. They had been running inventory on the food stores.

As he and the others entered the cell block, Jericho felt a bright sting of relief to see that the empty cell on the corner was now occupied. She stood up as they entered, climbing off the bed. They could all see the nanite injection site on her neck— the complex circular pattern of metal filaments was distinctive. It looked exactly like the ones on his wrists, Bruges's tentacle, Pavel's leg, Phaedra's back, or Sadiki's hands. Jericho sighed and looked away. That hadn't taken Fang long.

The girl didn't say anything—maybe she couldn't, because

when she saw Bruges, she attempted to sign, her arms waving in an approximation of his tentacle language. Bruges averted his eyes. He couldn't sign—it wasn't allowed. None of the rest of them spoke it fluently, but they avoided using what they did know. Bruges didn't want to be reminded.

They washed up in the shower room. Soap had not been allowed since the time they'd used it to blind the droids and attempted an escape. Once they were sort of clean, they filed into their cells. The moment they entered cells the force fields that made up the cell walls pinged into place.

Jericho finally worked up the courage to look at her just at the lights flicked on and off indicating that lights out was imminent. She was standing in the middle of her cell, still dressed in the floor-length blue medical gown, her left shoulder was a massive green bruise, and her red braids were now mussed and in disarray. She looked lost, scared and at the point of tears. And there was nothing he could do about any of that.

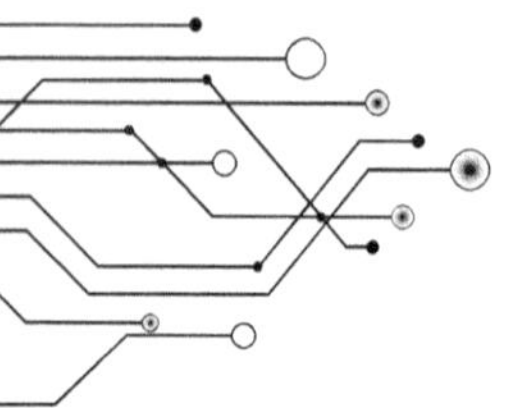

Chapter 6

KEELIA LANDS IN THE FIRE

Once the lights went out, it was like being back in the med-tube. There were no external light sources. She stepped forward and stubbed her toe on the force field, which spent sparkles of light shooting across the field and a sharp jolt of pain up her foot. None of the others said anything, though for a moment she thought she saw the black-haired man across from her look in her direction.

Who were they? What were they? Prisoners like her? They were all locked in cells, but no one had made them enter. What leverage could make someone do that? Gingerly, she felt along her throat. There was something there. And even worse, she would swear that something moved when she touched it—something underneath her skin.

She carefully backed up until she found the bed, and then she sat down.

Three men, one woman and an Octoparian. Octoparians were generally a quiet race but absolutely deadly if crossed. It was very difficult to fight eight arms at once, and their flexible bodies made it difficult to hold them in place. Of the humans, the oldest man looked like some kind of accountant, but the other three looked like they would be difficult to take in a fight. The youngest, a brown-haired man-boy about her age, looked like a Goran Eight belter, and they had a reputation for swearing, drinking, and fighting—not necessarily in that order. The green-haired woman—she could've been from any number of planets—had broad shoulders and an easy way of moving that Keelia had seen in the best fighters. The black-haired man looked the least modified, but the tattoo she'd seen on his forearm in the med-bay identified him as one of the Blue Band. They belonged a galaxy away with the Chimera Compact. The Alliance had tangled with them before, and the results had not been in favor of the Alliance. What could keep one of them here? What could keep any of them here?

Keelia lay back on the pillow and felt along her throat again. The same thing that could keep her here, she supposed. But that didn't explain why they wouldn't look at her or talk to her.

It was a long time before she slept, but when she did it was with troubled dreams of insects marching across her motionless body. When the lights snapped on, she felt as if she had barely closed her eyes.

Keelia sat up, rubbed her eyes and looked around—nothing had magically changed while she slept. She instinctively ran a hand across her hair and realized that it must be a disaster. She took the hair ties out and ran her fingers through it, combing out the snarls as best she could. Then she braided it and used the second tie to put it up in a bun and out of the way. She looked up and realized that the black-haired man was watching her. He looked away as soon as she made eye contact. She was tired of this. They could at least acknowledge each other.

"H—" The word she had intended to make was cut short before it had even escaped her mouth. The searing pain in her throat stopped it before she could make a noise. As she blinked away tears of pain, she put her hand up to her throat—there was definitely something moving there.

The walls of the cell dropped with a sizzling sound and Keelia looked around as the other prisoners emerged. Perhaps now they would talk to her?

The door to the cell… room? suite? Block? Yes, the man had called it a *block* in the med-bay. She was really going to have to learn his name. Whatever it was, the door opened and three robots buzzed in. The other prisoners froze, eyeing the robots with dislike and suspicion.

Fang and Kodor entered next. In her hand, Fang was carrying a black object trailing wires and Keelia felt her heart sink. Fang had found the emergency kernel of the *Black Light*. Every emergency kernel would send a distress call and a profile of each of the people in need of assistance. The fact that Fang had it meant that it was no longer active and that Fang now knew who she and her brothers were.

"Did you think I wouldn't find out?" demanded Fang, ignoring the other prisoners and coming directly to her. "I know you think I'm stupid, but you will learn that I am smarter than anyone you have ever met." Fang grabbed Keelia by the chin. "You're going to learn that I am not to be toyed with." Keelia hadn't been intending to toy with Fang or anyone. "But you appear to want to learn the hard way."

Keelia grabbed Fang's hand and yanked herself free. She tried to talk again, but no words came out. At least there wasn't any pain this time. Fang chuckled at her discomfort and Keelia settled for making a questioning, confused gesture.

"You can stop pretending," said Fang, holding up the kernel. "I saw the profiles. I know you're not stupid. I know you're an engineer."

Keelia wanted to protest that she wasn't fully licensed. But then realized that probably in an un-populated quadrant, while faced with a mad-woman, that the fine line of licensure probably didn't really matter. She shrugged and nodded.

"Good," purred Fang while stroking her shoulder, but either failing to, or choosing not to realize it was the injured shoulder. "Good. We have a use for engineers. Come along."

Keelia attempted to stay where she was, but every step Fang took and every step Keelia didn't take, increased the pain burning in her throat. Finally, she gave in and followed Fang out the door. This time she didn't look back at the other prisoners.

"This," said Fang as they arrived in a lab, "is your new office. Isn't that nice? You get an office. Don't you like me now?" Keelia pointed to obvious blood spatter on the wall covering the ever present Nazari Corporation logo. "That was Steve," said Fang. "Never mind about him. I'm sure that won't happen to you. You can have it cleaned if you want."

Keelia looked back at Kodor, who was hunkering nervously in the doorway, as if he didn't want to come in.

"And here," said Fang, pulling her by the hand to a window that overlooked a clean room, "is your problem."

Inside the room, on long tables were trays and trays of broken shards. On the farthest table, some of the pieces had been reassembled into a flat wall and tiny bit of a corner, possibly leading into a cube shape, but there wasn't enough assembled to tell for certain. The bits were tiny, silver gray, and covered in writing. But still, reassembling should have been well within the capabilities of the computer.

"I need you to put the pieces back together again. It's very important."

Keelia pointed at the computer. A first-year graphic design student should have been able to figure this one out. Why would Fang think she needed an engineer?

"Go ahead," said Fang. "Try it."

Suspiciously, Keelia flipped on the computer, familiarized herself with the diagnostics array and typed in her command. The room was filled with a strong blue light as the computer scanned the interior of the clean room. The results flashed on the screen.

Clean Room A421 contains zero samples.

Fang laughed as Keelia scratched her head. "There's nothing wrong with the computer," said Fang. "It just won't recognize that material as existing. Your job is to put the thing back together again. And I expect results. The last few engineers weren't up to the task. I hope you'll have better luck."

Fang swept from the room. Keelia waited, but no one returned. She ventured to the door and found two robots waiting for her. They beeped as she approached and extended taser arms. She retreated back into the lab and looked around. She began flipping on equipment and computers. Eventually she found a blank tablet and took it out to the robots, writing as she went.

Bring me breakfast and a maintenance droid to clean my office.

There was a whirring between the robots and eventually one of them blinked acceptance of the command.

Keelia went back in and stared into the clean room. They looked like simple archeological fragments that she could simply go in and puzzle piece them together. It was low-tech, but it could get results. On the other hand, things didn't get placed in a clean room behind airlock doors without some expectation that they would be dangerous. The lab central computer finally finished booting up and the AI face formed in a beam of light above it.

"Hello, I'm the lab AI—Crystal. Are you my new engineer?"

Keelia held up the tablet. YES, I'M KEELIA.

"Oh, good. I like new engineers. Would you like to record? The others liked to record."

HOW MANY OTHERS HAVE THERE BEEN?

"Five. Irina, Steve, D'ana, Hi-niss, Fresia."

WHERE ARE THEY NOW?

"I don't have the data to respond to that."

WERE THEY ALL WORKING ON THE OBJECT IN CLEAN ROOM A421?

"There are no samples in Clean Room A421."

Keelia frowned. Obviously, the blindness extended beyond the scanners. She tried again.

DID THE OTHER ENGINEERS ALL SPEND TIME IN A421?

"Yes, they spent on average seventy-two percent of their lab time in A421."

I WOULD LIKE TO SEE STEVE'S LAST RECORDING.

"No problem!" said Crystal cheerfully.

Her image was replaced by a small image of the office interior.

A man was pacing the length of the office, a small laser drill in his hand. He seemed to be muttering to himself.

"They will all understand," he said, speaking loudly for the first time. Then he squatted down and rubbed the floor. "Or maybe they won't. I can't be sure. Crystal!" He stood up and spun around, to face the central computer. "Crystal, baby, talk to me. Tell me you have results!"

"There are no new results," said Crystal. He giggled and clutched at his mouth.

"OK, that's fine," said Steve, patting the computer. "I know you did your best." Then he put the drill in his mouth. Keelia averted her eyes as Steve activated the drill, but she turned them toward the blood spatter on the wall.

The recording finally ended and Crystal came back on. "So," said Crystal, cheerful as ever. "How can I help you today?"

Nevertheless, the girl firmly resolved to redeem her brothers, even if it should cost her her life. She left the hunter's hut, went to the middle of the woods, seated herself in a tree, and there spent the night. The next morning she went out and gathered asters and began to sew. She could not speak with anyone, and she had no desire to laugh. She sat there, looking only at her work. After she had already spent a long time there it happened that the king of the land was hunting in these woods. His huntsmen came to where the girl was sitting.

Jacob and Wilhelm Grimm, The Six Swans

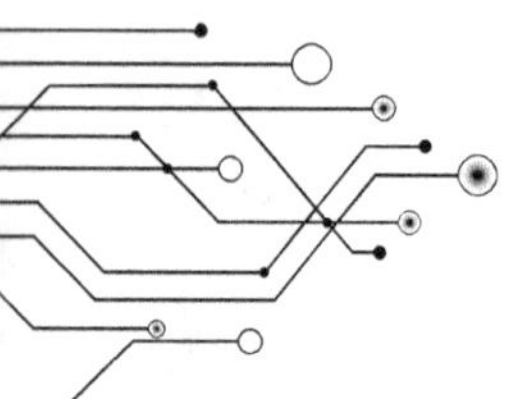

Chapter 7

JERICHO HAS A CONVERSATION

The girl didn't eat with them. She didn't work with them. The only time they saw her was in the few minutes at the end and beginning of every day. She never spoke, and after a few attempts to sign with Bruges, she gave up even attempting communication.

At one point, he tried to leave clothes in her cell, but the droids hadn't allowed it. Transfer of belongings was not permitted. Instead, she continued to dress in the floor-length blue medical gowns, periodically appearing in a fresh one. Perhaps that was all that Fang would allow for her. They were allowed a few minutes to themselves in the mornings to move between cells and eat—Bruges had suggested talking to her then, but Phaedra said there was no point because she would only go the way of the other engineers.

Theoretically, Jericho agreed with Phaedra. But every morning, the girl would wake up and work the tangles from her hair, combing it out with her fingers in a waterfall of fire, and he would lie in bed for a few extra minutes and pretend not to watch. Then a set of droids would come to the door and escort her away. In the evening, he would sit on the floor of his cell and toss a ball at the wall just to watch it spark and wait for her to return. He told himself he wasn't really waiting. That he just happened to be sitting there. It was a cell, after all. Other than hiding in the partitioned off toilet area, there wasn't any place that he wouldn't see her.

Every day for a month, he promised himself that he would be doing something else when she came back. And every day he couldn't find anything else to do.

He was sitting on the floor again, throwing the ball when she returned as usual. But instead of climbing onto the bed and pulling her feet up under her medical gown, she waited in her cell, standing in the middle watching the droids leave. Then she came close to the wall and sat down across from him. It was closest she'd ever come to him, since the first day. Now only six feet and two force fields separated them.

She waved and he found himself waving back. He felt stupid. After a month of living together, this was the closest they had come to communication.

She reached inside her gown and pulled out a stack of what looked like cut up pieces of a previous medical gown. She put them in her lap and held one up.

WHAT'S YOUR NAME?

He cleared his throat, suddenly nervous. "Jericho. What's yours?" Her expression dropped into chagrin and she stared down at the pile in her lap. "Didn't write that down?" She shook her head. "Next time," he said, and she nodded.

DID MY FAMILY ESCAPE?

Family. Not crew. Family. Strong word choice.

"Yes," he said cautiously. "They used the star's gravity and pod thrusters to sling-shot themselves out of the quadrant."

She beamed.

"But… they still only had twenty-four hours of oxygen."

She waved that away and almost hugged the slip of paper the question had been written on.

She held up the first question and pointed around the cell block, although she had only partial visibility of Bruges and none at all of the others.

"Phaedra, Sadiki, Bruges, and Pavel," he said. She nodded, then sorted through her pieces of papery fabric.

WHAT HAPPENED TO IRINA, D'ANA, HI-NISS, AND FRESIA?

He noticed she didn't list Steve. Maybe she knew what happened to him already.

"They're dead," he said. There wasn't any point in hiding it. "Irina and D'ana committed suicide. Fang killed Fresia. Hi-niss… may have been trying to escape." Or it might have been another suicide.

She looked thoughtful, but not surprised.

DO YOU KNOW WHAT I'M WORKING ON?

He shook his head. "No, Fang won't let us into the labs." He didn't add that there were too many things that could be used as weapons in the labs. She looked disappointed and pulled out some of the papers, setting them aside.

WHERE DO YOU GO EVERY DAY?

"Most days we go to the mines," said Jericho. She stared at him, perplexed, then made a sign that he didn't recognize. "I don't know what that means."

"Wants to know what we dig for," said Bruges.

Jericho snorted. "We don't know." She looked even more confused. "Fang won't tell us. She only tells us to dig. Phaedra thinks it's the galaxy's largest diamond."

"Phaedra hopes," corrected Phaedra from further down the row of cells.

"Bruges does not speculate without evidence. Sadiki thinks it might be an artifact from the first Alliance." At this, she looked thoughtful, tucking one hand under the opposite elbow and lifting that hand to her face. She tapped one finger against her lips. "And Pavel is *fjandinn* tired of talking about it."

"Yes, I *fjandinn* am," yelled Pavel from the cell next to Bruges.

Tap, tap went the finger on her lightly pink, perfect lips. Then she pointed at him. An obvious inquiry as to what he thought. He didn't want to say what he thought because he hoped what he thought wasn't real. He was saved from having to answer by the flash of lights that indicated lights out was imminent.

"Last call," said Jericho. "One more question?"

She sorted madly through her pile and held up a last sign.

THANK YOU.

The room went black and he was grateful. He didn't want her to see his face. She might as well have slapped him. *Thank you.* What did she have to thank him for? The only thing he'd been able to do for her was keep her from falling into the exhaust turbines. And he wasn't entirely sure that wouldn't have been better than leaving her alone with whatever drove engineers mad up on level four.

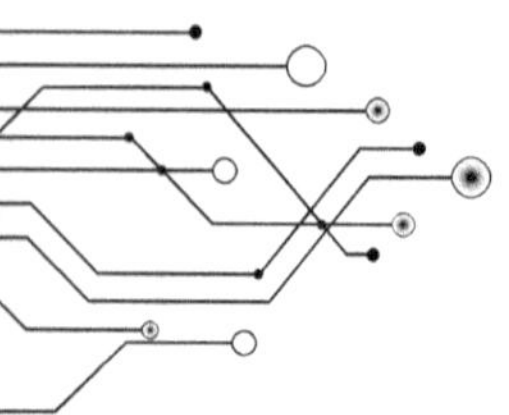

Chapter 8

KEELIA REVEALS HER TEMPER

Keelia restrained herself from bouncing up and down and waving like an idiot when she saw Jericho step off the lift. The droids wouldn't let her leave the lab area, but she hovered in the doorway and watched as he wheeled the mechanical arm off the freight elevator. Her excitement tamped down when Fang followed him out of the lift a moment later, but he winked at her as he came through the door.

To have him here was the culmination of a week of work on Fang. But it had taken her twice that long to decide what she wanted to do. And every day that had slipped by had seemed like one more day wasted. But her father's advice to her in school stood her in good stead here.

Watch, observe, act upon data. Don't always follow your first instinct.

It had taken Keelia weeks to skim through the recordings of the previous engineers. Each engineer had begun to exhibit signs of paranoia and irrationality approximately one month after visiting the clean room for the first time. She couldn't tell if it was the quantity of visits to the room, which was an average of twelve, or the time span of one month, but either way she sliced it, going into the clean room resulted in a frighteningly rapid descent into talking to people who weren't there, drooling, laughing inappropriately, and suicide.

They had left behind other artifacts. The computer engineer had hacked Crystal into being much more helpful. Crystal could now direct droids on minor errands, alert her when someone entered the lab suite, and had low level access with other databases throughout the complex. Which was how Keelia learned that the thrumming she felt in the deck plating under her feet was the engine that pushed the entire asteroid through space. Which, in turn, made all the careful astronomical data the astronomical engineer had collected utterly useless. She also knew that this would make it harder for her family to find her, but fortunately the civil engineer had left her a half-completed plan to attack the engine cooling system. It was a stupid plan, but it did give her access to that system. It was short work to cause a tiny leak that would leave a trail of ion gases. She implemented the plan and hoped that it wouldn't blow the system, which seemed to be held together on a roll of duct tape and a prayer. All of the systems seemed to be in some sort of state of disrepair.

After assessing the previous attempts to reconstruct the box, Keelia began to formulate her own plans. Fang had a tendency to pop in for *chats*—if you could call torture a chat—and soon Keelia was going to have to show some actual progress. After the last visit from Fang, Keelia had been forced to send a droid to the med-lab for a suture kit. Fang had sliced through the skin of her arm simply by raking at Keelia with her inhumanly hard finger nails. Keelia had been late getting back to the cell block as a result and Jericho had been pacing. She liked that he worried. Although he did seem to have more influence than the others with Fang, she knew there wasn't much he could do if she were to actually get hurt. But, still, it made her feel like she mattered to someone.

The problem was that all artificial intelligence refused to see the material in the clean room. The solution to that was to create a simulacrum of the pieces and then have the computer reconstruct the parts. But since she didn't dare go into the clean room, the problem became: how to make a copy? The solution, when she arrived at it, was something the other engineers had considered, but dismissed as too time consuming and not necessary. She required the installation of a mechanical arm and controls. Not so complicated mechanically, but incredibly difficult to get Fang to agree.

"I don't know why this is necessary," complained Fang as Jericho lowered the arm into place. Keelia, under the support frame, ran the bolt gun home, screwing it into place.

"Well, it's been two months and she hasn't started drooling," said Jericho. "Maybe she has a plan."

"Or maybe she's just lazy," said Fang. "And this is her way of pretending to make progress."

Keelia finished bolting the arm into place and crawled out. She typed a quick message on the computer next to her.

"I will have two pieces added by next week," Crystal read for her.

"You'd better," said Fang. There was a ping and the nanites in her dress chittered. "We've arrived at the outer beacon. Border patrol wants a word with me."

"I'll go with you," said Jericho.

"So you can try to pass secret messages again? I don't think so." Fang looked at Keelia and smiled. "I know, why don't you stay here and hang onto her for me?"

Automatically, Jericho's hand latched onto Keelia's wrist.

Keelia looked down in surprise and tried to pull away, but couldn't. Fang giggled, then turned to leave.

For some reason, it enraged Keelia that she was being used to slow Jericho down and on impulse she threw the bolt gun, still in her other hand, at Fang's head. The gun never made it to her—the dress swallowed it and spit it out. Fang whirled around towering over both of them.

Refusing to be cowed, Keelia held up her arm with Jericho still attached and gestured angrily at it and then to the new mechanical arm.

"Oh, is he getting in your way?" Keelia nodded. "Really? Tsk. So sad. Jericho, put both arms around her."

Keelia managed a meep of surprise and Jericho enveloped her in a hug and then winced in pain as whatever was in her throat punished her for the noise. Fang laughed. "I'll be back. Try not to get too comfortable."

"Really?" said Jericho, as the door closed behind Fang. "You just thought you'd chuck it at her head?"

Keelia swatted at his beard where it was tickling her face and tried not to look embarrassed. Her temper always got her in trouble. Slowly, his arms relaxed and more distance was allowed. She eased back and pushed at his arms, indicating that he could let go, now that Fang was no longer with them.

"I can't," he said, impatiently. She raised an eyebrow. "For the same reason you can't talk." She stared at him. She hadn't been able to bring that stack of questions back to the cell block yet. "Nanites," he said. "In my wrists."

Keelia felt a surge of excitement, and whirled around in his arms to grab his wrists. Her examination of her own mark had been awkward and inconclusive. She'd guessed some sort of nanites, but she hadn't been able to confirm. He had his hands over each forearm and she pried them off, trying to get a closer look at the marks on his wrists. The same circular silver filament pattern marked each wrist, but outward from it was a crazed pattern of scarring something like stretch marks, but slightly raised. She pushed his arms up higher to get a closer look.

"No! Don't!"

She got as far as chin level and his arms slammed her back into his chest, pinning her there.

"They thought you were trying to escape."

She twisted her head to try to look at his face. Judging by the scarring from the nanites he had a lot more experience with them than she did. And it was true that the nanites seemed to react to her thoughts. Potentially, they could then form theories about her behavior. But how to adjust their theory? Carefully, she angled her neck and pressed it against his forearm. It was an awkward position and ended up with his hand half-buried in her hair. She concentrated on how she did not want to escape, that she liked it right here, but she was curious—just curious.

His arms relaxed until they dropped into her hands.

"How did you do that?" he asked as she lifted his arms to inspect them again. "Did you really make your nanites talk to mine?"

She looked over her shoulder at him and shrugged. The scarring was oldest and thickest near his wrists, but continued up his arm. She tried to pull up his shirt to look further, but the sleeve only went up so far.

"There's some on my chest if you really want to see."

That was helpful. She unsealed his shirt halfway and pulled it open. She found the light scar pattern on his chest. She was disturbed that it didn't follow the vein pattern. It had on his arms. Why not here? In fact, here it seemed to form a different pattern entirely. Why the change? There was something here she wasn't seeing.

Chapter 9

JERICHO FINDS SOAP

The huntsmen, however, not letting themselves be dissuaded, took her to the king.

The king asked, "Who are you?"

But she did not answer. He asked her in every language that he knew, but she remained as speechless as a fish. Because she was so beautiful, the king's heart was touched, and he fell deeply in love with her. He put his cloak around her, lifted her onto his horse in front of himself, and took her to his castle. … "My desire is to marry her, and no one else in the world." A few days later they were married. Now the king had a wicked mother who was dissatisfied with this marriage and spoke ill of the young queen.

Jacob and Wilhelm Grimm, The Six Swans

She was tapping her lip again and staring off into his space. At the same time, her left hand rested on his chest, her thumb running over his scar repeatedly. He tried to keep his breath shallow, hoping she wouldn't notice, waiting to see what would happen when she did.

She turned her head, as if she was about to start a sentence, and saw her own hand. She blushed scarlet and snatched her hand away, backing up as far as his arms would let her. He tried not to laugh.

"Did you come to any conclusions?" he asked. She shook her head and avoided eye contact. Then she pointed toward a work bench across the room. She didn't wait for a reply, but started walking, which was a disaster. They arrived at the bench tripping and bumping into each other.

"Well, that needs work," he said, feeling out of breath. He couldn't tell if it was from the awkward dance of getting there or the simple fact of her body smashing into his.

She nodded, but pushed his arms onto the bench and began grabbing things out of the cupboard above. He barely had time to register that she'd pulled out a very large needle when she jabbed it into his arm.

"Son of *tik*!"

She withdrew the needle and plunged it into a gel puck. He stared at the puck.

"Did you just extract one?" he asked. She slid the puck under a scanner. The AI displayed a tiny bug looking thing on the screen. He was overwhelmed by a feeling of hatred. "Can you extract all of them?" he asked.

She half turned and shook her head sadly. Then she typed a something on the tablet on the work bench.

"Maybe I can learn to stop them if I study them," said the computer, reading her words.

Jericho stared at her, trying to decide how to react. None of the other engineers had taken the slightest bit of interest in any of the rest of them. Because of that, it had never occurred to him that they might be useful. "How can I help?"

More typing. He leaned over her shoulder to look, wanting

to read it instead of having the computer talk for her. He didn't know what her voice sounded like, but he knew it wasn't the smooth, flat tone of the computer.

I don't know yet.

He was disappointed, but this was more than he'd had a moment ago. She pointed across the room and started to walk off.

"No," he said, pulling her back. "I'm not doing that again." He picked her up and she looked down at him slightly bemused as he toted her across the room. He set her down, lowering her gently, and unintentionally running his face along her neck.

"Oh, Gods below," he groaned. "You smell like soap." He stood up rapidly and pulled back, feeling himself flush. She looked startled. "We don't get soap anymore." He stumbled over the words. She cocked her head inquisitively and he took a deep breath. He felt like an idiot. Probably about the same as she had a few moments ago. "Are we even yet?"

She grinned, her eyes crinkling in her silent laugh. She typed a few commands into the nearest computer and then turned back to him. She pointed to her hair and then to the sink on the far side of the lab. There was a small dispenser of soap next to it— intended for hand washing.

"You wash your hair in the sink?" he guessed. He sighed, unintentionally voicing his jealousy, still eyeing the sink. She reached up and touched his head and then pointed at the sink.

"No," he said wistfully. "I probably shouldn't." Her face very clearly expressed a lack of understanding on his reasoning. "I mean, it would be awkward…"

She rolled her eyes and started walking, pulling him along with her.

"Please stop doing that!" She glanced back and paused, waiting for him to catch up. He positioned himself by her side, his arms still around her, like a complicated partner dance. He kept eye contact with her and this time they started off at the same time, arriving at the sink in a few smooth steps. "See? Better."

She tried to look unconvinced, but he saw her smile. He faced the sink and once again reconsidered whether or not it was a good idea. On the other hand… soap. She reached out and brought out the extending spigot arm and he found himself obeying her. It took a bit of complicated geometry to arrange themselves, but he was soon leaning over the sink as she scrubbed his hair. He tried not to rub his head against her fingers like an affection-starved pet.

She finished rinsing his hair and he stood up, flipping his hair back behind him, enjoying the feeling of water running down his back. He opened his eyes and looked down at her. She held up a hand towel. "Let it drip," he said.

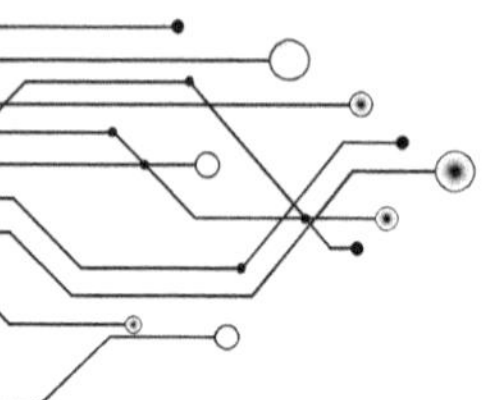

Chapter 10

KEELIA SHOWS JERICHO HER WORK

He opened his eyes and smiled at her and Keelia found her stomach doing flip-flops. She had always thought he was good looking. Probably. Under the beard somewhere. But smiling down at her with those dark eyes and his arms around her… She was suddenly short of breath. She offered up a towel because she had nothing else to do and standing there smiling at him like a moron probably wasn't good. But he didn't want it.

"You have no idea how much better this feels," he said, looking around the room and beaming. If he had been one of her brothers, she would have laughed at him. But she did not feel at all sisterly. She found herself remembering the hardness of his chest and the ease with which he'd moved her around the room. She looked around also, trying not to make eye contact, hoping that he wasn't secretly telepathic.

"What *are* you working on?" he asked suddenly. She looked up—his expression had changed to a frown. He was staring at the mechanical arm and the clean room.

She relaxed. Work. She could talk about work without being an idiot. She went to show him the clean room.

"No, no walking off without me," he said pulling her back again.

She mouthed, *sorry,* and waited while he positioned himself. Then they walked across the room together. She picked up a tablet and wrote a quick note.

"Sorry—" began Crystal, reading for her, but he cut her off.

"Computer, I'll read for myself."

"No problem!" said Crystal cheerfully.

Sorry. I forget to think before acting. It's a problem.

He grinned. "But I'm guessing mostly just for other people," he said. She shrugged, but felt pleased at his reaction.

She typed a few more sentences and held up the tablet again.

Fang wants me to reassemble the box in that room. But all the other engineers who handled the pieces went crazy and committed suicide. So I don't want to go into the room. That's why I needed the arm.

"Why didn't any of them just get a mechanical arm?"

Keelia hesitated.

Using an arm is a hard skill. And I don't think they had much space experience.

"Space experience?" He frowned.

It's a wide universe full of dangerous things.

She was repeating her mother with this one. It was true, but she wasn't sure what to add to get her point across.

"Mm." He grunted slightly. "No one thinks they're safer than someone who has never seen danger."

She nodded.

I don't think they understood that 'just pieces of metal' could do what they obviously do.

"Sounds right. To be honest, they were all kind of arrogant little twats."

Keelia nodded again. That was definitely her impression. When she had been in school, she had been snubbed by many of her fellow students. Most of the engineering student body was comprised of children of the rich from the inner planets. The idea that someone from the outer reaches would travel inward to get a license was acceptable, but everyone knew those students were sub-par—the equivalent of poor relations. It had upset them very much when she had out-scored and out-performed them on every test.

Keelia had realized quickly that she wasn't necessarily more intelligent than the other students. What she had was actual boots-on-the-hull experience and a genius for a father who had never once assumed that because a discipline wasn't his, that it was useless.

It was her estimation that the five deceased engineers suffered from the same locked-in way of thinking, utter lack of experience in space, and complete disregard for the things a well-honed group could achieve. Although they had been captured much the way she had and had each spent some time looking for ways to escape, they had all virtually ignored the other prisoners and approached their escape attempts solely from the point of view of their specific engineering disciplines: astronomical, structural, civil, biological, and computer.

"What's this?" he asked, pointing at her drawing board.

Each piece of the box has equations on it. These are my notes from the pieces I can see. I can't tell if the pieces have individual equations on them or if it's one long continuous expression. I probably won't know until I get it put back together. But I thought if I could solve some of the maths, I could tell what the purpose of the box was.

"So, you're going to work on nanites, solving complex equations and putting an ancient artifact back together?"

And escaping.

"Sure," he said, grinning. "Why not?"

It's not like I have anywhere else to be. What else am I supposed to do with my time?

"Good point."

He seemed about to speak when Crystal interrupted him. "Fang has exited the lift on this floor."

"Quick," he said, obviously changing what he'd been about to say. "Write your name."

Keelia's fingers seemed stiff and slow as she typed her own name and held up the tablet.

Keelia Black.

"Nice to meet you, Keelia Black," he whispered, just as the door to the lab suite opened. She turned around and pretended to work on the equations in front of her, ignoring him.

"What happened to you?" demanded Fang, looking at Jericho's wet hair.

"She dumped a glass of water on my head," he said, and Fang laughed.

"Good girl," said Fang, patting Keelia's cheek. She caught sight of the math and began to peruse the board. "You failed to carry the integer here," she said, pointing.

Keelia stepped back, colliding with Jericho, and mentally cursed—Fang was right. Embarrassed, she erased up to the mistake and began to correct.

"I expect better results than this," said Fang sternly. "Jericho, for Gods' sake, stop holding onto the poor girl."

Jericho let go of her with a sigh of relief, and Keelia tried not to feel a little bit hurt. He rubbed his shoulders and she realized that he'd probably been more uncomfortable than she had been.

"Don't stare like an idiot," said Fang. "Keep working." She waved at the board, and reluctantly, Keelia did as she was told. "Come along, Jericho. You have work to do too."

Keelia watched them go, or rather, she watched him. For the first time, she found herself ignoring Fang entirely.

Chapter 11

JERICHO THINKS OF HIS FATHER

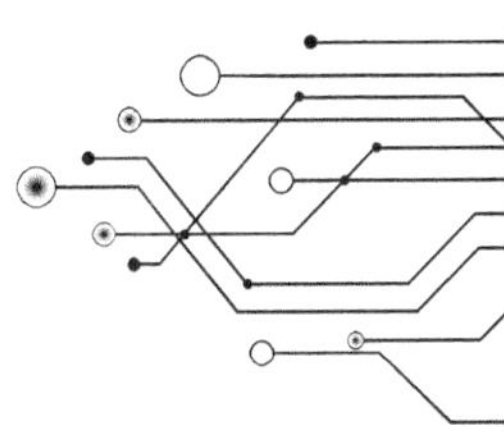

Fang had finally agreed to take them to a trade planet. It meant a lot of paperwork and talking to bureaucrats. Most people didn't fly a small moon around. It raised questions—about where to park it if nothing else. And since Fang didn't answer questions, it meant that Jericho spent a lot of time pretending to be Jericho Nazari, princeling of the Nazari Corporation. When he had been in the military, he'd despised the part, only assuming it at his father's occasional request. He found it even more constraining now. He squeezed into the role of a normal person like a large man in a small suit. He couldn't remember how normal people talked or acted anymore.

Keelia helped. When he talked to her, he remembered what it was like to not be forced to do anything. She arrived every few days with a fresh stack of notes tucked under her gown. And she asked questions, endless questions, most of which he didn't have an answer for. He loved when he did, because her face would light up. His absolute favorite was when she would start to think and then turn to him with a fresh question and say his name. She never made any sound, and she always looked sad and frustrated immediately afterward. He didn't enjoy that part, but he liked the way her lips looked around his name.

He wasn't the only one being affected by her. Everyone chatted more now in the evenings. Sometimes to each other and sometimes chiming in with answers to Keelia's questions. Bruges had even translated for her a time or two when Jericho couldn't figure out what she was asking. The only one who remained silent was Sadiki. Jericho had no answer for that. He suspected that even if he somehow managed to get them all free, Sadiki would never be quite the same person that he had been before Fang.

Now, three months after Keelia's arrival, Fang had summoned Jericho to the top most level of the base. He was rarely allowed up to level one anymore—it housed all the entertainment zones, guest suites and his father's old office. Plants lined every wall, freshening the air, adding color and softening the hard metal walls and floor. Fang's style—even before she had modified herself—had always been austere, and now it was as if she no longer even cared to have even the smallest of human comforts. Level one was the last remnant of the old Fang. Everything on level one was softer, lusher, more luxurious, but for him, every trip upward was like a visit to a past he didn't recognize anymore.

He stood on the plush carpet that the cleaning droids would probably have to sanitize after he left and stared at the portrait of his father—Marid. Growing up, most people had said he looked more like his mother. Maybe now that he had a beard, he looked more like Marid. He really didn't know—he had stopped looking at himself in the mirror a long time ago.

Staring at the portrait, he remembered his father stomping around their estate in rubber boots. "This is where your great-grandfather built the first Nazari house. We're descended from Gwynn Flaxenhart herself, you know. But your great-grandfather knew that being the fifth son of a fifth daughter meant he would never be more than a TenDek corporate stooge. So he took the buy out and came out here to build this!" Marid had beamed at the rickety shack. "The second year here, the valley flooded. He worked through three days of non-stop rain and hurricane winds, building wall after wall of sandbags. In the end, the flood waters came within one foot of the doorstep. Everyone else on the delta had to rebuild." His father, with his big barrel chest and hands on his hips, stood proudly on the front stoop of the Nazari homestead, staring across land that now belonged entirely to him. In his mind, that's how Jericho remembered his father: beaming and proud.

Jericho had been happy when his father had married Fang. She was a weapons developer in one of the Nazari company labs, and they hit it off almost immediately. Fang was glamorously pretty, but more importantly, she was smart. Marid had finally found someone he could talk to and who was passionate about the same things he was. That was enough for Jericho; he liked seeing his father happy. For five years Jericho and Fang had enjoyed a respectful, if not affectionate, relationship and then he'd joined the military and at some point in the next dozen years, something had gone wrong. Jericho had sensed it in his intermittent visits home or the scattered calls with his father, but he'd kept putting off asking. His father always handled things. It was really none of his business.

And then his father had built this place. Marid started talking about his obsession for the ancient relics almost exclusively. And somewhere between the battle of Vers'nd One and the stand at Fortis Four, his father had died. Jericho had come to the base for the first time, expecting to escort his father's body home. Instead, he'd found an almost unrecognizably modified Fang, and he'd never been permitted to leave again.

The door to his father's office opened and he saw Fang pacing inside.

"This is your fault," she said as he entered.

"What is?" he asked patiently. Fang was taking more side-steps out of sanity lately. He was hoping that at some point she'd be crazy enough that he'd be able to kill her. The danger was that she'd go over the edge and take them all with her.

"It's all these distractions. I can't think properly with all these distractions. I would have finished it weeks ago, but all of you distract me."

"Finished what?" asked Jericho, eyeing her dress. It was thrashing in agitation.

"The new weapon for the Board. I should have had it by now. The Board doesn't understand what I'm up against. It's not my fault."

"Right, we distracted you," said Jericho.

Fang slapped him. Which was rare. She rarely hit anyone herself and Jericho was surprised by how cold her hand was. He put his hand up to his cheek, trying to rub away the chill.

"I didn't mean that," said Fang, breathing hard. "I know you're working on the artifact. You don't mean to distract me, but I have to keep working."

Jericho watched Fang carefully. He felt as if he had been dropped into a scene halfway through and didn't know any of his lines.

"The artifact," he said, inching out over a deep space of

Fang's mind on a tin-foil bridge. "We'll be at the center of the asteroid soon. Will it be there?"

"Of course it will," she said impatiently. "And I know you think that it will be a whole *new level of weapons technology*, but we can't wait that long! The Board needs results now."

"What will the Board do?" he asked.

"That's what I'm trying to tell you! They're sending a representative! We can't have that!" She chewed at a finger nail. "But I don't see how we can prevent it. And I swear I can get it done in time. If only that stupid girl would help me." Jericho felt his chest tighten as he tried to keep himself from reacting.

"This is your fault." She had looped back around again. "You brought her here. And I know, I know…" She teasingly wagged her finger at Jericho. "She's doing great on your artifact project—three pieces this month alone! But I'm telling you, she's useless on the development side."

Jericho was starting to get a sick feeling in his stomach.

"What are you developing?" he asked. Fang hadn't so much as gone into her lab in over a year. He had hoped that was permanent.

"The sonic blaster," she said, as if he were ridiculous. She tapped a few commands on the desk and the screen brought up an image of her lab. The drill that had been brought in from Keelia's ship was in pieces on the floor and her work bench was obviously in use. "I swear you're getting forgetful. And I admit I haven't spent much time in the lab lately, but I haven't slipped that much. I can get this done before the Board rep gets here. It's the differential that's giving me trouble. If that stupid girl would just tell me how she solved it in the prototype, I would be home free."

"Who is the Board sending?" asked Jericho cautiously.

"Some idiot named Thanh? Trang? I don't know. I wasn't listening. You'll take care of him, won't you? You're always better at those people than I am."

"Yes," said Jericho, feeling a surge of hope. Thanh had been an ally of his father's. If he could get Thanh's help, they might be able to take down Fang. "I'll take care of Thanh. She'll expect to be wined and dined a bit. It's a good thing you decided to pull into the trade planet. We'll be able to take on supplies."

"I can't think about that right now," she said impatiently.

"I'll take care of it," said Jericho.

"Yes, good. Do that. I have to work."

"Yes," agreed Jericho, backing toward the door. "I'll make sure no one bothers you. You need to concentrate."

His hand was on the door knob. A few more feet and he'd be out of the room, with direct orders to go get supplies and talk to Thanh.

"Thank you, Marid," she said as he softly closed the door.

He clicked the door closed and stood on the other side, trying not to let go of the scream of absolute anger he felt welling up. Taking a deep breath to steady himself, he jogged to the lift, trying to get off the level before she clicked back around to reality.

Chapter 12

KEELIA DOES AND DOES NOT MAKE PROGRESS

Keelia stared at the graphite powder and worried. The magnetic field aboard the base was shifting. It should shift a bit—they were traveling into a new orbit after all. But this… This was not shifting a little bit. She spilled another teaspoon of the graphite and watched it settle into two circles, like a figure eight or an infinity symbol. It was getting stronger. Two weeks ago, before she'd added the most recent piece of the box, the effect had been limited to the space immediately outside the clean room. Now it was in the outer lab.

Her solution to getting pieces of the box together had been ludicrously low tech. A large sheet of paper on top of the pieces and then she had used the mechanical hand to rub graphite powder over the top. The computer had then been able to scan the rubbings. When reassembled, each box wall would probably be a little over the length of her forearm. But whatever had smashed it had shattered it completely, and the biggest piece was no more than the size of her thumb. Some of the pieces were still covered in space residue or dirt, and some still had purchase tags on them. Whoever had gathered the pieces had gone through an enormous amount of effort. But once she had the rubbings, the computer had been able to assign numbers to all the pieces and spit out a list of instructions on how to reassemble it. If she wanted to, she could put together an entire wall of the box in the next few hours.

She stared again at the double loops. Keelia was not at all sure that putting the box together was a good idea.

Once again, her thoughts turned to her father's drill. If she turned it on, couldn't the family find her before Fang did anything disastrous? Fang didn't know about the uplink and she was interested in the tech itself, not in the Swan Clan. Maybe Keelia could just tell Fang what she wanted to know and it would be all right. She looked at the calendar that she made Crystal keep on permanent display. It had been three months and six days since she'd arrived. The family had to be looking for her by now. Couldn't they find her quickly?

Unless her family hadn't found Niall and the others. They might not even know she wasn't with her brothers. The idea that no one was looking for her set off a cascade of nerves in her stomach.

If she was wrong, if her family wasn't close by, then she would have just exposed a world of inventions and technology to Fang. And Fang seemed to only use new technology to hurt people. Specifically, the five people Keelia saw in the cells every night.

Keelia stared at the filings again and considered her next move. She couldn't help thinking that if Niall had been here, he would have had an escape plan well in motion by now. Easton and Graves would probably have done some telepathic voodoo and had everyone out by supper. Or Anwell… Well, if Anwell had been here, he probably would have blown up half the base by now, but technically that would be an escape. She wasn't sure what Jed and Matty would have done. As a medic, Jed had firm feelings about killing people, but Keelia was pretty sure he'd be figuring out a non-lethal solution to Fang. Matty would probably try to figure out how to fly the asteroid base some place useful.

In some ways, the previous engineers had been like her brothers—each looking at the problem from their specific area of study. D'ana, the deceased biological engineer, had left some interesting theories on the nanites behind before going bonkers and throwing herself into the exhaust shaft. Keelia's close questioning of Jericho had led her to some thoughts of her own on that topic. The nanites were extremely legalistic—they followed the letter of the instructions given to them. The other prisoners had, to Keelia's complete lack of understanding, been forced to sign contracts with Fang and the nanites enforced the contracts. It was what compelled the other prisoners to return to their cells every night, as sort of base code of instructions that could not be crossed without extreme pain. D'ana's theory was that the nanites could be redirected to a different Home Database—her word for Fang—with alternate contracts. Keelia didn't see why the nanites couldn't simply be blocked from accessing the Home Database at all, which should render the nanites inert. Keelia was working the problem, but her progress was slow. She needed something with a biological component and organics were not her strong suit.

Her next option was gaining access to the droid programming. Steve, whose remains no longer decorated her wall, had made progress in that department. With Crystal's help, he had carefully mapped the programming levels and loops of the base robots. He'd theorized that if someone were to work within the droids' core programming and loop that, they might be tricked into helping with an escape. But Keelia lacked the hacking skills to make that happen.

Freesia had come up with a plan to blow the CO2 scrubber unit on the theory that it would force Fang into going somewhere for repairs. Keelia wasn't entirely sure that Freesia's maths were correct and rather thought that they might just end up blowing half the base instead. Keelia knew she could settle down and get to work checking that, if she really wanted.

Keelia sighed and went back into the lab with Crystal. The truth was that everything she did felt slow and nothing she did seemed to get her anywhere. If she didn't have Jericho to talk to, she would have given up and given Fang what she wanted by now. But watching Jericho resist Fang day after day made complaining about three months of silence seem a bit whiny.

The thought of Jericho steadied her and upended her at the same time. In the month since Jericho had been forced to put his arms around her, she'd only been able to talk to him across the barrier of their cells. Keelia had initially told herself that it had simply been the proximity of his body that had made her react so strongly. But the feeling hadn't gone away. He could make her heart do back-flips simply by smiling at her—which she went out of her way to make him do. She could tell that he was used to looking after people. He took care of the rest of the prisoners— that much was evident from the snippets of conversation she heard. But she couldn't tell if he was simply taking care of her the same way or if he actually felt anything for her.

Keelia looked down at the medical gown, which was all that she could get the droids to bring her and wished that she could at least have some real clothes and a little makeup. She knew she was being ridiculous. She was stuck in a prison. She had plenty of work that could be done on getting the hell out. Not to mention that there was a strong possibility that she was working on an alien artifact that was affecting the magnetic field around her and had the power to drive people insane. And instead of worrying about any of that, she was mooning over a man who couldn't remember to shave and probably cared more about soap than he did about her and really only talked to her at night because he was just a nice person.

Keelia had taken a deep breath and was trying to resign herself to solving more equations when Crystal flickered to life.

"Two of the guard robots have exited the lift and are heading for the lab," she said. "The deployment database indicates that they were instructed to come by Fang Nazari."

Keelia bit her lip. That didn't bode well. She hit save on all of her work. If things went terribly awry, at least the next engineer would have a better briefing than she'd had.

The droids entered the lab, wheeling on their single orbs. It was a design that only worked on the smooth-floored space bases. With their slightly tapered cylindrical bodies, they looked like exclamation marks. The display on their chests flashed with their orders: *escort Keelia Black.*

Reluctantly, Keelia followed them from the lab. They took her to the lift and then up two levels. The layout was similar to her lab, but had more work space. It reminded Keelia of her father's workshop. Disassembled bits lay scattered around and abandoned boards of equations sat next to each project. Keelia also couldn't help noticing the dust that lay over most of the surfaces. The lights were on above the center work bench and that was the only clean area. Her father had sometimes jokingly referred to his workshop as his spider web that he continuously filled in and added to and which could not be disturbed without him rushing out to investigate. But this web was being slowly abandoned, the owner retreating space by space, withdrawing into the center.

Fang was waiting for her, standing in front of the work bench with a black apron over her dress. In front of her, an oversized gun sat on the work bench, connected by a tether to a tablet that she fidgeted with. Keelia realized that the hulk of metal parts on the floor next to the bench was the remains of her father's drill.

"The pre-sets should work," said Fang, slamming her tablet down in frustration. "It's the differentiator. You're doing this on purpose."

Keelia stared at her mutely.

Fang turned to her with a smile. "Would you like to see how I've improved the design? Don't answer that. I know you're dying to." She took Keelia by the arm and pulled her closer to the work bench. "Your idea was good, but so prosaic. And really, does the universe need another way to crush rock? For Gods' sake, just make your slaves have more children if you need to go faster. But killing someone? There's always room for a new way to do that. You can see I've made it compact enough to be carried—if you get one of those giant lunkheads or a Kodor. Everyone should have a Kodor, really. I keep forgetting to patent his design." Fang looked around as if expecting to find Kodor lurking. Keelia felt fortunate that for once he wasn't. He had a tendency to lick his jowls too much when Keelia was around. "Did I ever tell you that I got him out of a *Grow Your Own Reptile Kit?*"

Keelia stared at Fang in horror. Every kid had a *Grow Your Own Reptile Kit.* They had produced an endless amount of iguanas, turtles and snakes throughout the known universe. Matty still had his tortoise. There was no way that Kodor should have been able to be produced by one of those.

"Well, it was several kits combined," said Fang. "And of course, I did the genetic work myself. He's a bit of a genius considering what I started with. I wanted to market him, but the Board said he wasn't useful. I wonder if I could sell a *Grow Your Own Kodor* with every gun? That would seem practical. If you have a heavy gun, wouldn't you want a henchman to go with it?"

She seemed to want a response, and Keelia offered a strained smile and a shrug. Cheerful Fang was almost always followed by angry Fang. Fang seemed to consider the marketing possibilities of a Kodor plus Gun.

"Or it could be mounted on a mechanical of some kind. Either way is fine." She waved away the mobility considerations and focused on the gun again. "I've given it pre-sets. They should work. Or you could put in a genetic sample here." She pointed to a small sense pad on the side.

Keelia felt her dream of switching on her father's drill shatter into a million pieces. One of the reasons she'd wanted to become an engineer was so that she could understand her father when he started babbling. Unfortunately, it worked all too well. She knew exactly what Fang was saying. Fang had taken the concept of the drill—targeting a specific rock type and pulverizing it by disrupting the atomic bonds through sonic waves—and applied it to people. Now Fang could target a specific person or group of people simply by getting a genetic sample. And she already had a Black family sample.

There was no way Keelia could turn on the drill now. The Black family would be walking into a trap.

"But the problem," continued Fang, "is that it doesn't *fjandinn* work. So, you're going to tell me what you did to the differentiator on the prototype and then I can make mine work."

Keelia swallowed hard.

"Well, go on," said Fang, gesturing impatiently. "Speak."

"I did not program the drill." Her voice creaked and grated as she stretched muscles unused in months. She coughed at the unaccustomed sensation and then tried again. "I don't know how the differentiator works." It wasn't a total lie. She didn't know for certain what her father had done, but she could take a pretty good guess. It was similar to something they'd worked on together a few years ago.

"Lies," said Fang, slamming her hand down on the work bench. "The label is quite clear. It is a Black Device. You are Keelia Black."

"There are a lot of Blacks," said Keelia.

"Tell me what you did!" screamed Fang, her dress surging upward so that she towered over Keelia.

"No," whispered Keelia.

The pain was instantaneous and burned along her neck like it was on fire.

She didn't know how long the pain went on, she only

remembered repeating *no* and Fang standing over her screaming. Or maybe Keelia was doing the screaming. It was hard to be certain.

"That's enough!" bellowed Jericho.

He pulled her off the floor and she couldn't figure out how to stand up. She clung to him and tried to remember where her feet were. This was not the way she'd wanted to touch him again.

"This is none of your business," said Fang, breathing heavily.

"She's working on the artifact," he said. "That's important."

Fang blinked rapidly. "Yes," she said, her breathing slowing. "Yes, the artifact. That's important. But you know I have to have the weapon done by next month. She can't be allowed to slow me down."

"You don't need her," said Jericho, pushing Keelia toward one of the droids. "Don't get sidetracked by her."

"But she built the prototype," protested Fang, caressing Jericho's arm.

"That you are improving on," he said.

Keelia clung to the droid and finally found her feet. She looked back at Fang and Jericho.

"You can come up with something original," Jericho added confidently.

Fang was stroking Jericho's beard and nodding, while staring intently at her gun.

"I know she's your pet," said Fang. "But really, I will only be patient so long. You know what we're up against. If I can't figure this out soon, she has to tell me. You understand?"

"Of course, I do," he said soothingly.

"I know, I know. Of course you do. Who else would? I know that you and I are in this together. But I'm starting to think the others are against me." She sounded petulant.

"Don't think about them," said Jericho. "You just need to let me worry about them. Ignore them and don't let them distract you."

"Well, I would, but your stupid girl won't give me what I want!" Fang rounded on Keelia, clawing at her arm and shaking her.

Jericho pried Fang away, taking the insane woman's hand and holding it gently. "You don't need her," he said softly, kindly. "You're smarter than she is." Fang leaned against him, putting her arms around him with a sigh. "I'll take her away, so she won't distract you anymore," said Jericho soothingly, putting his arms around her and patting her back.

"You're always so good to me," said Fang, straightening up and smiling at Jericho with a sweetness that Keelia had never seen before. "You always know just what to say."

"I'll take her away," said Jericho again, backing up.

"Yes," Fang said, waving her hand dismissively. "Take her back to the lab."

Jericho half-carried her back to the lift.

"What the hell are you thinking?" he demanded savagely when the lift doors closed. The droids clustered around them. He tilted her head to inspect her neck and she pushed his hand away. Even if she had been able to talk, her throat was now so inflamed that she doubted she could get a word out. "You cannot do that," he said. "She will kill you. Do you understand?"

She didn't respond, staring angrily at the flicking level counter above the door.

"Why the hell didn't you just tell her how to work the damn drill?"

She pulled her gaze away from the numbers and stared at him. How was she even supposed to respond to that?

"It's just a drill. Next time she asks, tell her how it works."

The door opened and she pushed past him, stumbling into the lab suite. He was working with Fang. He was helping her, working with her. He was going to get her family killed and he didn't even care.

He was stopped outside the lab suite, blocked by the droids, and she was relieved.

That night, she waited until the last possible moment before letting the droids take her down to the cells. The lights were flickering as she stepped into her cell. He was waiting for her.

"Keelia!"

She refused to turn around and went straight to her bed. The lights snapped off and there was a starburst of light and a hard sizzle as he slapped the cell wall in frustration.

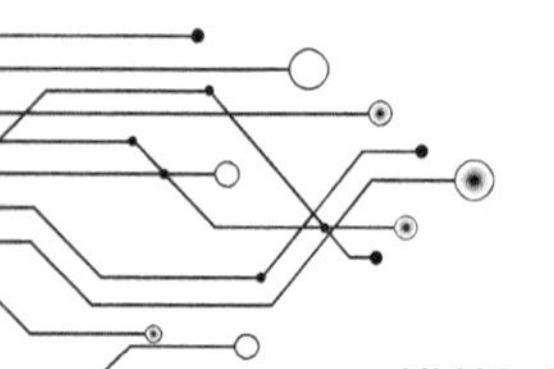

Chapter 13

NIALL AND THE BLACK SWAN BROTHERS AWAKEN

Niall awoke to the pinging sound of far off gun fire. His pod was open and the air was full of mist or smoke. He coughed on the fumes, tried to sit up, and failed miserably. The ceiling had some sort of strut work. It didn't look substantial enough to be a ship. Grasping the edge of the pod, he hauled himself upright and looked around. The room felt… odd. The nearest wall looked made of pre-fab metal sections, but the far wall looked like it was made of some sort of mud. He shivered as a strange chill swept the room and as he watched the smoke move he realized that it was under the effect of an atmosphere. The strange chill had been wind. It had been a long time since he'd been on any planet. He'd forgotten what it felt like. His brother's pods were lying on the floor around him. Some were on transport beds. It was as if someone had been in the process of moving them and then wandered off.

He took stock of his body. His arm was still clearly under the effect of the Aurora Fungus, which was probably for the best because it looked like it would hurt if he could actually feel it. There was a lot of dried blood down his arm and he could see a metal shard sticking through. He was going to have to do something about that soon. He half-climbed, half-fell out of the pod, only to realize that the pod was on a table before falling the extra three feet down.

He pushed himself upright and staggered to the closest pod.

He activated the opening sequence and went to the next one. By the time he'd gotten through the other four pods, Easton was emerging from the first. The fumes, whatever they were, were still dense, but starting to dissipate.

Easton looked around, taking stock.

"Mom is here somewhere," he said.

"Good," said Niall. "We could use the help."

Anwell was next, then Graves, popping up like a jack-in-the-box.

"Anwell, watch the exit," ordered Niall. He went back to Jed's pod. Of all of them, Anwell fought best when impaired. He claimed it was because he had honed his animal instincts. Matty claimed it was because Anwell spent the most time impaired and was therefore more practiced. Niall rummaged through Jed's emergency bag as Jed began to blink and wake up.

"Blek," said Jed, opening and shutting his mouth. Niall ignored him, still rummaging through the bag. Jed reached up and began to shift the sleeve around on Niall's arm—not that he could feel Jed's fingers, but he could see the movement in his peripheral vision. Niall ignored the sense of panic that went with that sensation and lifted the adrenaline out of the bag. He prepared to inject a dose into his arm.

"Don't," said Jed grabbing his hand.

"It won't wake up," said Niall.

Jed stared at him and Niall could see from his face that it was bad news.

"It's not going to," said Jed. "It won't wake up because the tissue is dead and no longer connected to you. You lost an artery.

The heat from the sun's corona seems to have heated the metal and cauterized the wound for you, but if you hit it with the adrenaline, the arm will start to rot. Right now the fungus is the only thing keeping infection from setting in."

Niall swallowed hard. He looked around the room. He had to get his brothers out. He had to find Mom. And he had to get over the fact that he'd just lost his arm.

Matty was climbing out of his pod. They all looked unsteady on their feet. Easton and Graves looked the most awake, although Graves looked like he needed a hug. That was probably because Niall needed a hug.

"Easton, Graves, on recon. Figure out what's out there, find Mom if you can, and get us some weapons. Anwell, Mat back them up. If you can, find us a computer and a way out."

The four of them slithered through the door, keeping low. Jed climbed out of his pod, still inspecting Niall's shoulder.

"Do you know how we woke up?" asked Niall, submitting to his brother's inspection.

"Um," said Jed, looking around the room. "Dad. Probably."

"Yes, Easton said Mom was here," said Niall. "What does that mean? What is this fog? Should we be breathing it?"

"Yes," said Jed. "I think it's Substance 248 gas in the building's ventilation system. Apparently, it was originally a gas-form biological weapon. Dad thought that meant the antidote could be aerosolized, but we hadn't gotten around to trying it."

"Great," said Niall.

Jed's com dinged with an update. "We've been out for about three months," he said.

"I needed the sleep anyway," said Niall.

There was the sound of fighting. Niall and Jed froze, waiting.

"Three rooms beyond are clear," said Matty, leaning back into the room. "We're moving forward."

"Right behind you," said Niall.

"I'm not sure you should be moving much," said Jed.

"I'm not sure we have a choice," said Niall.

Jed grunted and held the door open for him. The next rooms looked like some sort of sorting rooms. Long tables held a massive collection of things that were being shuffled into bins: weapons, clothing, jewelry, devices. Anwell and Matty were digging through the weapons bin. Three heavily modified humans were dead on the floor.

"Crap, crap, crap." Anwell tossed weapon after weapon aside.

"Got one," said Matty and tossed a pistol to Niall.

"I'm going to have learn how to shoot port paw," said Niall.

"You do that half the time anyway," said Anwell. "You are monumentally annoying on the topic of training evenly."

"Anwell!" snapped Jed.

"It's an arm," said Anwell. "It's tragic, but as long as he's alive, I don't really care how many limbs he has." He thumped a crossbow against Jed's chest. "Now stop whinging about what an asshole I am and help us get out of here."

"You really are an asshole," said Jed.

"Of course he is," said Mat. "That's why we always send him out first. An, you want this blast staff or this gun?" He held up the options.

"Blast staff," said Anwell, grinning.

"Anybody know where we are?" asked Niall.

"Easton thinks it's a Rantarian Slave Mart," said Mat. "Come on. They went this way."

Niall grunted in dissatisfaction. Rantar was a resource-poor planet with huge deserts periodically punctuated by jagged mountains. The native Rantarians—if there was such a thing anymore—had at some point in their history turned to selling each other to the highest bidder. A habit that, over the centuries, had become the main industry on the Gods' forsaken ball of rock. There were six major slave marts on the planet—sprawling, massive conjoined buildings incestuously building on and over each other—and a multitude of smaller markets around the planet. Some markets specialized in slaves only, while others took in junk from space and offloaded it for parts. The markets didn't do quite the trade they had now that the Alliance had returned, but they hadn't been put out of business either.

Anwell and Mat led the way through a series of interconnected rooms. The place was hot and humid, even as the gas dissipated and Niall found he was having trouble breathing. There was an argument going on ahead of them, which wasn't unusual for his brothers, but it was unusual between Easton and Graves. The twins almost never argued and certainly not verbally where everyone could hear.

The room was crowded with stuff that looked bizarrely like props for a theater. A human-sized birdcage occupied one corner.

"What's going on?" demanded Niall, and Easton and Graves broke apart.

"Easton is not listening to me," said Graves. "We need help. This place is a maze and he can't get us out."

"I can help," said a woman. Niall looked around. He had been so focused on his brothers and breathing that he hadn't noticed the woman in the cage.

"We don't need your help," snapped Graves.

She was wearing a blue dress and her dark curly hair was clipped tight to her head. She had warm sepia skin and well-muscled arms. She might be tall, but it was difficult to tell due to her seated position.

"I can get you through the maze," she said. "They have a scatter net up. You're not going to be able to do it alone."

"I believe her," said Graves. "But Easton isn't listening."

Niall assessed his brother. Easton was sweating and had the far-off look that meant he was existing elsewhere. "Easton, look at me," said Niall, leaning against the woman's cage. Reluctantly, Easton turned his head in Niall's direction. "Focus on me, please." Niall watched his brother's gaze sharpen. Easton blinked and looked around. "Easton, have you found Mom?"

"No," said Easton unhappily. "I think there's a scatter net... Someone just said that didn't they?"

"Yes. If you can't find Mom, then we need help," said Niall. "Can we trust her to help us?" He pointed to the woman in the cage.

Easton focused on the woman. "Yes," he said again, unhappily.

"Good. Matty, Anwell, get her out."

"I'm going to need some things first," said the woman.

"Like what?" asked Niall, clenching his fist around one of the bars.

She pulled her dress aside. "Well, like my leg for starters." Niall stared at the metal cap on her thigh. It was clearly intended to receive a cybernetic leg.

"Any idea where it's wandered off to?" asked Anwell.

"Anwell!" snapped Jed. "Seriously!"

"What?" asked Anwell, clearly at a loss for what he had said this time.

The woman looked amused. "In the next room there are two black boxes. They're both mine. Bring them to me and I'll help you get out of here."

Anwell looked at Niall, who nodded. Anwell and Mat ran from the room.

Looking pale, Graves abruptly sat down on an upended box.

"Jed," said Niall. "I'm going to need something here. It's starting to wake back up around the edges."

"What do you mean?" asked Jed, peeling away Niall's shirt, to take a look.

"He means it's *fjandinn* hurting," yelled Graves.

"Sorry, Graves," said Niall, "I'm working on it."

"Jed, do something," barked Graves.

"Graves, go help An and Matty," said Niall, staring at the far wall trying to shut down the pain that was driving Graves crazy. Jed pulled a piece of Niall's shirt away and Graves did as he was told, running from the room. "Easton, how are you doing?"

"It's fine," said Easton, approaching the cage with a heavy looking mallet. "I'm blocking you."

Easton slammed the mallet against the door lock and the woman stood up and hopped ungracefully to Niall's side of the cage, out of the path of the door or mallet. Niall grunted in pain as Jed injected him with something. The woman put her hand on his and he found himself looking up into the prettiest pair of brown eyes he'd ever seen.

Anwell and Mat returned toting two boxes. Graves hovered in the doorway. One was almost four feet across and six feet long. The other seemed to be about the size one would expect for a leg. Easton hit the door once more and it sprang open with a clang.

Anwell and Mat carried the boxes into the cell and opened the smaller one.

Niall heard the excited intake of breath from the woman. She reached in and lifted out the leg, fitting it into place. It was high-polished silver and looked—well, he wouldn't have wanted to say it out loud, but it looked sexy. She stood up, settled her dress into place and then stepped to the second box. The box opened and she pivoted as two wings seemed to jump out at her and latched onto her back. Reaching into the box again, she pulled out a massive gun.

"Where do I get one of those?" asked Niall.

"You have to lose a limb," she said.

"Working on it," said Niall.

"Come see me after, then," she said. "All right, boys," she said turning to the rest of the brothers, her wings fluffing out. "Who wants to blow the *skit* out this place?"

There was a sizzle as Anwell's blast staff lit up. Niall tried to laugh and then winced. "When do we not want to do that?"

An hour later, the building was in flames and the slave traders who ran the place were mostly dead. Niall considered whether or not to try and follow his brothers or whether or not he should sit and wait for them here, wherever here was. There was the flutter of wings and the woman landed in front of him.

"The landing bay is up ahead a little ways," she said.

"That's good," said Niall, sitting down on a pile of rubble and leaning against the wall. "I'm just going to take a little break."

"You've probably earned it," she said.

He made a grunt of disagreement, but didn't respond otherwise. He let his head rest against the wall.

"Hey," she said, kneeling down in front of him. "So there's six of you and there were six life pods brought in with the Nazari Corp logo on them. Was that you?"

"Yeah," he said.

"They said everyone inside was dead?"

"Appearances can be deceiving," he said.

"Do you work for the Nazari?" she asked, her head tilting a little, trying to maintain eye contact.

"No, she's who we escaped from."

"She?" The woman's expression intensified. "Let me guess, a crazy *tik* with turquoise hair and a dress that moves on its own?"

"You've met?" he asked, trying to pay attention.

"Not yet," she said. "But I fully intend to introduce myself." Her expression said that it would not be a pleasant meeting. "I was on my way to find her when I got a little waylaid here."

"You do know she has her own moon base and an army of droids?"

"That's about what I've heard," she agreed.

"Did anyone mention the seven-foot-tall man-alligator thing?"

Her expression suggested that no one had. "Doesn't matter," she said with a shrug. "She killed a friend of mine."

"A friend?" His expression must have been skeptical because she looked annoyed.

"Look, you may have gotten out with all five of yours—which, good for you—but I don't have so many friends that I can afford to lose one."

He laughed softly and shook his head. "There's supposed be seven of us."

"You lost someone?" she asked, her head cocking inquisitively.

"My little sister," he said. "Have to go get her once we're done here. And then we will explain to Fang Nazari why you should not mess with the Black family."

"What are you going to do when you find her?" asked the woman, looking amused.

"Hadn't quite decided," he said, his eyelids beginning to drift lower. "Sometimes the classics are the best."

"Classics?"

"Rip off her head, spit down her throat." He hadn't meant to say that out loud. The civilized peoples of the galaxy rather disapproved of that sort of sentiment. But she chuckled.

"Ah. I guess by *classics*, you mean the old ways. I can get behind that."

"You're welcome to come along," he said, letting his eyes close.

"Thanks. I might do that." He didn't respond. He was finding it harder to think. "Hey!" she said sharply and his eyes snapped open. "So that's tomorrow," she said. "What are you doing for the rest of the week?"

"Oh, you know," he murmured. "The Black family usual. Pissing people off and getting in fights."

"Sounds fun," she said. "Hey Niall, maybe you should stay awake."

He opened his eyes. "I didn't get your name," he said.

"Tara Carbanado," she said with a smile.

"That's pretty," he said, closing his eyes again.

"No, Niall, come on, keep talking to me."

"No, it's fine," murmured Niall. "I'll just take a little nap. The guys have got it covered. They don't need me."

"Um, no," said Tara and he felt her hand against his neck, feeling his pulse. "No. I think you should stay awake. Come on. Open your eyes for me."

He did as she asked, but it was hard. She smiled at him. There was a sharp explosion and Tara grabbed her gun and spun around. Niall put his gun down.

"Hey, Mom," he said, falling over.

"Hi, honey," she said bending over him, her hair swinging around her chin in a red arc. "Got yourself into a bit of a pickle, didn't you?" She looked back over her shoulder. "Declan!"

"I lost her, Mom," said Niall. "I lost her."

"We'll get her back, baby, don't worry. Declan, I swear to the Gods—"

"I'm here," said Declan hurrying up and unpacking his medical bag.

"Jed says I'm going to lose the arm," said Niall.

"Well, you shoot left handed a lot anyway," said his mother.

"Go get Dad," said Niall. "You and Anwell suck at sympathy."

Tara leaned over him, her wings forming an arc behind her head. "I know where you can get a new arm. I know it's not the same, but I swear it's good."

He smiled up at Tara. She really did have the prettiest eyes. "Do I get the gun too?"

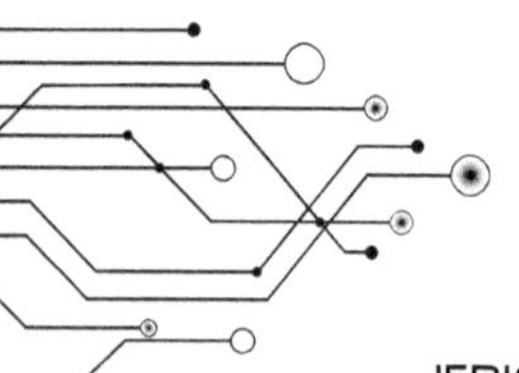

Chapter 14

JERICHO ARRIVES AT TETRAHINO TRADE BASE

Keelia had stopped sleeping facing toward him. In the mornings, she no longer combed her hair—she left immediately. There were no more questions, no evening chats. He wasn't sure how a person who couldn't talk could give him the silent treatment, but she was doing it. And it was killing him.

"You have to let it go," whispered Sadiki over the coms of their space suits as they rode the ore train out of the mine, preparing to dump the rock out onto the surface.

"It's a damn drill. I don't understand what I did wrong."

"You have to focus," said Sadiki. "Fang is slipping. We have to stay focused. We need to be able to take our opportunity when it comes."

"I know that," said Jericho, throwing a fist-sized chunk of rock at the wall, happy to see it shatter.

"You should cut your hair," said Sadiki.

"No," said Jericho. He couldn't quite put into words why the idea revolted him, but it was a line he couldn't cross. He had to have something that was his.

"You'll look more like Marid."

"No," said Jericho.

"The beard is working. But the hair cut would complete it."

"I'm not confused. I know why you want me to do it. I'm saying I won't do it. I'm going to have to shave anyway. The trade base we're coming up on is Primarian."

Sadiki clicked his tongue in disappointment. Jericho threw another rock.

"I'm going to have to put you all in the closet," he said.

"I know," said Sadiki.

"Are you going to be all right?"

"The others will be with me," said Sadiki.

That wasn't really an answer to the question, but Jericho guessed that it was the best that Sadiki could give him.

A week later, when the asteroid was in the designated orbit, and the security detail requested docking approach, Jericho went to get his friends.

The moon base had two registered human crew and one pet: Fang, Jericho, and Kodor. Anyone else would require registration. There would be questions. Fang wasn't so crazy that she didn't realize where questions would lead. The security detail that would scan the base could not be allowed to find the others.

In the core of the moon base was a central shaft that was impervious to scans. Below the basement level, where there was nothing but rock and pilings, there was a door into a small room built into that central core. Marid had intended it as a safe room and a place to smuggle brandy. Fang called it the closet.

He waited to get Keelia last. It went about as well as he had expected. She was not pleased. He held the door open for her and she stared at him in mute anger.

"Please," he said. "I have to put you in one way or another." He didn't specify what would happen if she didn't walk through under her own power, but she got the point. She squared her shoulders, raised her chin, and walked in herself. He wanted to smile—arrogance was against her character—but he didn't dare. She hated him enough already.

Once they were inside, he took himself up to his old suite on level one. It was like walking into a dead person's room. He didn't live here anymore. No one did.

He took a shower, with soap, and tried not to think about Keelia. He shaved, taking off layers of dirt and hair and when he was done, he still didn't recognize himself in the mirror. The nanite scars on his chest, the ones Keelia had touched, were twisted in a double loop like a figure eight. That was new.

He put on an old set of clothes. They felt soft and smooth against his skin—fancier, better, and no longer what he was used to—but he selected everything black. If he didn't get a chance to change back into work clothes, it was more sensible to wear black. The security detail escorted him to immigration to answer questions while they scanned the base. Fang remained in her workshop. The others remained in the closet.

He didn't even try to tell anyone at immigration he was being held prisoner. It was against his contract, and the nanites would try to prevent him, even if he managed to get the words out. He knew what would happen to the others.

He had exactly three hours from the time he left the immigration office to procure supplies. After that, Fang would start hurting people he loved.

Chapter 15

KEELIA AND THE CLOSET

A long time ago, a king was once hunting in a great forest, and he chased his prey so eagerly that none of his men could follow him. As evening approached he stopped and looked around, and saw that he was lost. He looked for a way out of the woods, but he could not find one. Then he saw a woman approaching him. She was a witch. …

After he had agreed to be married, the witch showed him the way out of the woods, and the king arrived again at his royal castle, where the wedding was celebrated.

Jacob and Wilhelm Grimm, The Six Swans

Keelia stood inside the door and felt nervous. This was the first time she'd been this close to the other prisoners.

"Oh, the princess got included in the party?" Pavel's sarcasm was biting. "I guess we should feel honored."

"Shut up, Pavel," muttered Phaedra, but it was half-hearted.

The room was about twenty feet across. Small for five people. There were two cots, and Bruges was pulling out glow lanterns from under the floor, snapping the seals and igniting their light. He handed them from tentacle to tentacle to Phaedra. She hung them from hooks on the wall. Sadiki was sitting on a cot, leaning against the wall, his eyes closed as if he was concentrating.

"Pavel, grab the blankets from under the floor, will you?" asked Phaedra. "We can't all sit on the cots."

"Why not ask the princess to get them?" sneered Pavel.

"Pavel!" snapped Phaedra.

"What? We're busting our humps keeping this rock in the sky and all she does is go upstairs and fiddle with computers and crap on Jericho. Like he's done anything but save her ass the entire time she's been here."

Keelia punched him. Pavel punched back. If someone had asked her ahead of time, she would have said that she expected him to. Belters had no sense of chivalry or at least no sense that a woman couldn't kick their ass. But since she had no plan to get in a fight with Pavel ahead of time, she hadn't expected anything.

The fight quickly turned into a wrestling match and Keelia knew what to do about that. She had six older brothers and a mother who believed in letting the children sort things out for themselves. She was behind him with her arms wrapped around his head and neck in short order. He bucked, trying to roll and she crossed her ankles around his waist and arched back—extending his body and tightening her grip on his neck. He made a glurging noise.

"You probably ought to tap, Pavel," said Phaedra leaning over them. "She's going to choke you out."

Pavel flailed and strained another few seconds and then reluctantly tapped her arm. Keelia kicked him off of her and stood up. Her dress was now torn and she felt like crying even though she'd won. She walked over to the darkest side of the room and sat down with her back to them.

Pavel and Phaedra argued quietly and Keelia tried to wipe a trickle of tears off her face without looking like she was. It had been three weeks since she'd told Fang *no* and her throat still hurt, but that wasn't what hurt at the moment. Eventually, Pavel and Phaedra stopped talking and Keelia was relieved. At least she didn't have to listen to their whispered conversation and pretend she didn't know it was about her.

"How long has it been?" asked Pavel after a while.

"An hour I think," said Phaedra. "He said he had three hours after he left the immigration office to get all our supplies. But I don't know how long immigration will take."

Silence reigned again.

Then there was a sigh and a thump as Bruges levered himself off the cot. He slithered over and sat down in front of Keelia, carrying a glow lantern. He set the lantern down and settled himself against the wall.

"You mad at Jericho—why?" he asked.

Keelia stared at him and then flailed her arms in the Octoparian sign language.

He wants me to kill my family.

Bruges's domed eyes rotated away in shock and then rotated back.

"I think no," he said.

He's working with Fang.

"No," he said firmly. "Stay calm, small human, start from beginning."

Fang is using a sonic drill my father created as a prototype for a weapon.

Keelia had to pause and switch from arm to hand signs. Octoparians could make very complex sign combinations, but she didn't have enough limbs to make all them. Fingers were a substitute, but couldn't quite bend the same ways. Fortunately, Bruges appeared to be able to work with her lack of flexibility, nodding along as she worked through the words.

She wants me to show her how the drill works so she can complete the weapon.

"Upsetting," said Bruges, when she paused.

If I turn on the drill, it will send telemetry to my father's lab.

Bruges's arms waved excitedly. "They could find us!"

If I turn on the drill, she will have access to my father's computer and she will know how to complete her weapon.

Bruges's arms dropped.

All the weapon requires is a genetic sample to target someone or some people.

"She already have sample," said Bruges, realizing her problem. One of his tentacles, rubbed over her arm sympathetically, the suckers making a sad little puckering noise on her skin.

Yes! It would be a trap for my family. And Jericho said I should give Fang what she wants. He's working with her.

Bruges waved his arms in distress.

"No! He no understand."

"What's she saying?" asked Phaedra.

"Fang want Keelia to make weapon. Weapon that kill Keelia family," said Bruges. "Jericho say give Fang what Fang want."

She said I was his pet. He hugged her!

Keelia emphasized her last sign with an extra thump.

"That's because she thinks he's Marid," said Sadiki.

With only two arms, Keelia might not have been able to make all the signs of the Ocotoparian, but she had *huh* figured out.

"His father," continued Sadiki. "Fang is his step-mother. She's getting worse. With the beard, she keeps confusing him for his father," said Sadiki. "It's how he got her to agree to let him go on the supply run."

There was silence in the room. Keelia wiped her nose and suddenly felt very stupid.

"But he said he was going to shave," said Pavel. "If he does that, is Fang going to start going back to her bitchtastic self?"

"He has to," said Sadiki. "Tetrahino is Primarian."

Pavel groaned. "We cannot catch a break."

"What's Primarian?" asked Phaedra.

"It's a religion. They don't believe in showing hair, so the men all shave and they wear a lot of wigs over their real hair," said Pavel.

Keelia made the *huh* sign again.

"Agreed," said Bruges.

"I can't explain it," said Pavel. "But if you've got facial hair they won't sell to you. It's like bad luck or the priest will punish you or something. Basically, if we want supplies he has to shave."

The shopping was a problem, but it wasn't germane to the situation. Keelia addressed Sadiki, who obviously understood what she was saying.

What happened to Jericho's father?

"Good question," agreed Bruges.

Sadiki looked uncomfortable. "Fang and Marid were married for nearly twenty years. Jericho was away in the military. I was Marid's lawyer. Marid found an ancient data drive describing an artifact and he became obsessed with it."

The artifact that I'm working on? The one that drives people crazy? Is that what's wrong with Fang?

Sadiki shook his head. "Marid was researching something he referred to as a Soul Sucker. He was convinced it could change the face of not just weapons technology, but all technology."

"Soul Sucker? Well, that sounds pleasant," said Pavel. "I'm sure nothing could go wrong there."

"Well, ominous nomenclature aside," said Phaedra, with a small chuckle. "What is it? Where's it from?"

"I don't know," said Sadiki. "Marid's first theory was that it was from the time of the first Alliance. But Jericho has seen more of his father's notes and he thinks it might be older and not human."

"So what happened?" asked Pavel. "Did Jericho's pop find this thing or what?"

"Perhaps," said Sadiki. "He purchased this asteroid and built this moon base on the theory that somewhere deep inside it was the artifact."

"Oh shit," said Phaedra, sitting down on the second cot. "That's what we're digging for, isn't it. No wonder Jericho never wants us to go faster."

But what about Fang?

"About the time that Marid bought this asteroid, Fang became increasingly erratic. She began to modify herself and work on the nanite technology."

The nanites are her invention?

"Yes. The dress was her first experiment with them. Does it matter?"

Keelia got so excited that her sign came out in a mush.

"Calm down, small one," said Bruges, petting her face with a tentacle. Keelia took a deep breath and tried again.

Yes! That means that the base code exists in the dress! If I could get a sample from the dress I might be able to figure out how they communicate with Fang and block them!

"I don't think that will happen," said Sadiki.

"It's not that far-fetched," said Phaedra thoughtfully. "I've stepped on them before. She loses them all the time."

"The hard part would be figuring out how to trap one un-damaged," said Pavel.

"We work on that in the not now," said Bruges. "What happen to Marid?"

"They had been living here about a year. I was attempting to get Marid to focus on some contracts that the Board wanted him to sign. He and Fang were arguing all the time. She was… not herself. Marid had gone so far as to mention divorce to me. I was more than happy to draw up the papers. I thought that without Fang he might leave this place and go home. One night, after dinner, I had returned to my room. I heard yelling and then Fang screaming. I ran out and Marid was at the foot of the grand staircase on level one. Fang said he slipped and fell. I wasn't there, so I don't know. But there was a crushed nanite under his body when they lifted it up. After that, it was as though the brakes had come off. Jericho returned for the funeral and when I tried to warn him, she locked me in here."

Bruges and Keelia both put an arm on Sadiki's knee and

Phaedra moved to his cot to hug him. Sadiki brushed them off looking embarrassed.

"It took Jericho six months to get me out. And he put the food, lights, and blankets in here, just in case it happened again. He is the target of most of her abuse, but also, I think the last link to her old self. She doesn't quite dare kill him. Jericho is not working with Fang," he said firmly. "This place used to be full of people. But humans who stay near Fang get killed. Jericho fired everyone he could to get them away from her, but Fang has been working her way through the rest of us. Jericho and I are all that's left of the original crew."

Why not just tell someone? Get help.

"When Fang was slightly less crazy, she invented contracts that everyone would have to sign. The contracts have a non-disclosure clause."

And the nanites follow the contract. That's so lame. Sad that I'm the only one without a contract and I still can't say anything.

"What?" demanded Sadiki. "You don't have a contract?" There was silence in the room as they all stared at Keelia.

"What do you mean, she doesn't have a contract?" demanded Phaedra.

Keelia looked around the room nervously. They suddenly all seemed very intense.

No, no contract. Why?

"No wonder the droids escort you everywhere!" Pavel looked excited.

This is good?

"Yes!" said Bruges.

"You can do things we can't," said Sadiki. "It means that Fang really is slipping. Our window of opportunity may be close."

But we need a plan. What are we going to do when the window opens?

"She want to know plan," said Bruges gloomily.

The rest of the room fell silent.

"We don't really have one," said Pavel.

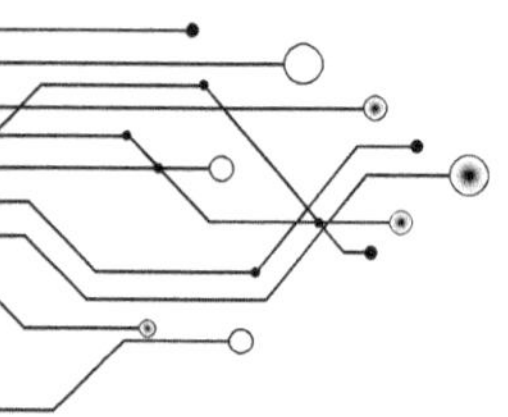

Chapter 16

JERICHO AND THE PLAN

Jericho opened the door to the closet and froze. Bruges and Keelia were holding hands, or tentacles, or whatever, her dress was ripped and she had a fat lip. Pavel had a black eye and obvious bruising around his neck.

"What did you do?" he demanded furiously of Pavel.

Keelia scrambled to her feet and began to sign.

"It terrible," said Bruges. "She trip on dress, punch Pavel in face."

Phaedra snorted.

"Yet another victim of a medical-gown mishap," said Pavel. "Truly tragic."

It was such an obvious lie that he didn't know how to react. Suddenly Sadiki began to laugh. He swung his legs off the cot and stood up with a stretch.

"Can we go now?" Sadiki asked.

"Yes," said Jericho. "I have dinner for us in the cafeteria." He moved aside to let Sadiki pass.

"Yay!" said Pavel, who squeezed out after Sadiki.

"Thank the Gods, you came when you did," said Phaedra, leaving next. "Pavel kept farting. I was going to let Keelia choke him out if he couldn't hold it in."

"Wait, what?" asked Jericho, but Phaedra was already walking away. He turned back to Keelia and Bruges. "What?" There was a flurry of sign, only some of which he could follow.

"Keelia like no beard. I disagree."

"I…" Jericho didn't know what to say. Keelia beamed a smile at him and tugged on his sleeve, pulling him into the hallway. He followed her.

"What'd you bring us?" demanded Pavel as they got in the lift.

"I ordered everything on the list," said Jericho. "Some stuff will have to be delivered, but we should be able to repair the cooling system tomorrow."

"Who cares about that? What did you bring *us*?" repeated Pavel.

"You were one of those kids that snuck out and pre-opened your birthday presents, weren't you?" asked Phaedra.

"Didn't everyone?" Pavel demanded.

"No," said Sadiki. "Only bad boys and girls do that and if the birthday fairy catches them they get nothing but engine grease for their birthday."

Keelia pointed at Sadiki in obvious and vehement agreement.

"Everyone knows the birthday fairy is your mom," said Pavel.

"You're getting engine grease," said Phaedra, as the doors opened.

"I am not," said Pavel, exiting the lift and leading the way to the cafeteria.

"Yes, Jericho brought you engine grease." Phaedra was firm on topic. "That's all you get."

"Take that back."

Keelia was giggling silently. Bruges waved his tentacles in confusion.

"He can't," Sadiki said. "You peeked and now the presents have turned to engine grease. It's the birthday fairy. There's nothing that can be done."

"Take it back," said Pavel. "It's not funny."

Keelia laughed harder, her shoulders shaking.

"No one is getting engine grease," said Jericho, stepping through the doors to the cafeteria. He was feeling too unsettled to find the teasing amusing. Sadiki was making jokes. Bruges was translating sign. Keelia wasn't mad at him. What the hell had happened down there?

He waved them in and gestured the escort droids to stay out.

"We're all getting booze and new socks." He pointed to the table where he'd dumped his pile of smuggled presents. He'd meant to surprise Keelia with socks as a peace offering. Her feet had to be freezing on the metal deck plating.

Keelia's eyes got big and she mouthed the word: *socks*.

"Booze," yelled Pavel and ran to the table.

"I actually don't know if I'll be able to give you socks," he said to Keelia nervously. "The droids wouldn't let me give you anything before."

Keelia wrinkled her nose in annoyance and signed something to Bruges. Then paused and spelled something out slowly. Apparently she didn't have the arms to complete *sub-routine*.

"Fang gave order for…" Bruges paused and then shook his head. "Maintenance? Solid maintenance?"

"It's a solid state sub-routine?" asked Phaedra. Keelia nodded emphatically and Phaedra grunted in annoyance. "That's impossible. That should never apply to a human."

Keelia nodded emphatically and signed again.

"Fang say *maintain Keelia?*" repeated Bruges uncertainly.

"What are you talking about?" asked Pavel, popping the seal on a bottle of Tetrahino Vodka.

"I think," said Phaedra, "that Keelia's saying that Fang ordered the droids to maintain her, but somehow that got translated to a maintenance sub-routine. Maintenance sub-routines all aim for original or like-new condition. You know how they hate when we start modifying stuff? Like the repair droid that kept having a freak out when we had to put the bitumen coating on the L7?"

"Son of *tik!*" said Jericho, realizing the problem. "They're trying to keep her in original condition, but as far as they know this is her original condition."

Keelia nodded.

"It's the degradation," said Phaedra. "It's moved to the droids. Something like that should never apply to a human."

"This place is going to kill us all," muttered Sadiki.

Keelia looked from Sadiki to Jericho, but Jericho didn't know how to explain that the moon base seemed to be falling apart around them. It sounded superstitious.

"Well, thanks for that prediction, Mr. Cheerful Pants," said Pavel. "But meanwhile, how do we fix that? Keelia can't go around barefoot forever."

Keelia shrugged and signed.

"It take long time to find problem," said Bruges. "Keelia not programmer."

"Well," said Phaedra, "for the immediate situation, we may be able to simply trick them. Keelia's feet aren't in plain view. If the droids don't see her get the socks, then they might incorporate the socks into her original condition profile like they do with hair growth. Essentially, they will think the socks grew on her feet. Of course, if we had access to the database we could reprogram her entire org-co profile. Or better yet, get them to stop applying the maintenance sub-routine to her entirely."

There was excited waving from Keelia.

"Keelia have that," said Bruges. "Skill she lacks."

"You have access?" repeated Phaedra, clutching at Jericho's shoulder.

Keelia nodded. Then held up two fingers to indicate how much. And then signed again to Bruges.

"No skill," he said again. "Need help."

"Oh, we can help with that," said Phaedra. "We are *so* going to help with that. But first, everyone line up in front of the door, so the droids can't see. Keelia, go grab some socks."

Keelia clapped her hands as they lined up and then dove into the pile and retrieved a pair of socks in a bright blue. She slipped them on her feet with an ecstatic sigh.

Pavel laughed and chugged out of the bottle. "Who wants music?" he asked passing the bottle to Phaedra. Keelia raised her hand.

"We should work on a plan," protested Jericho.

"We will," said Phaedra, downing a mouthful. "But first, we drink."

She handed him the bottle. Sadiki grabbed it before he could and took a drink. Jericho thought it was possibly the first time he'd seen Sadiki drink—ever.

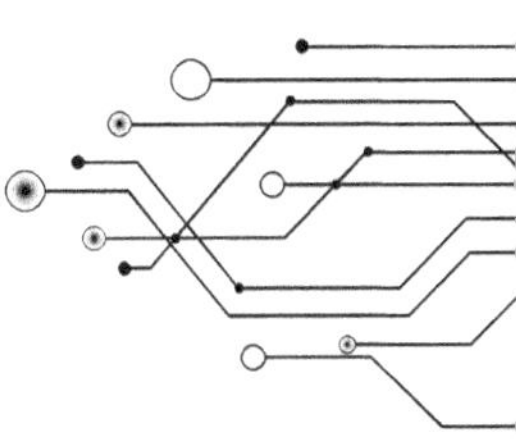

Chapter 17

KEELIA AND JERICHO IN THE LAB

Keelia sat on her bed and admired her blue socks as she brushed her hair with an actual comb—another present from Jericho. She loved all of her presents. She now had socks, a comb, a tablet of old-fashioned paper—which could not have been cheap—and a packet of charcoal that was intended for drawing, but she could use for writing, since all harder forms of writing utensils were not allowed in the cell block. Jericho had hidden them under the covers on her bed before the droids had seen them. She looked across the corridor to his cell.

His face was still mushed into the pillow. For once, his hair was down, and she could see that when standing it would swing past his shoulders. She wondered how long it had been since he'd bothered to cut it. She knew members of the Blue Band usually shaved their heads—she suspected that he must have been letting it go for several years. She went back to scrutinizing his face and realized that he had one eye open and was watching her in return. She suspected he was hung over—there had been a lot of drinking the previous evening.

She pulled her hair around, miming styles, soliciting his opinion. One braid, two braids, bun up top, two buns on each side, ponytail off her forehead? He grinned, laughing silently, and held up two fingers. She took that to mean two braids and began to part her hair with the comb. It was so much quicker than her fingers. She snapped the hair ties into place and looked up to realize that he was still watching her with a sleepy smile.

"Jer, you moving?" yelled Pavel from the wash room.

"No!" Jericho yelled back, then groaned and pulled his pillow over his head.

On impulse, she ran across the dividing space and pulled the pillow off, beating him with it.

"Gah!" He hid under the covers, and she laughed and whacked at the lump of him under the blankets. He snaked an arm out from underneath and knocked her over onto the bed, then reappeared to steal his pillow back. Keelia gamely tried to retain the pillow, but it was a losing battle.

"Ahem," said Phaedra. "Keelia's escort is here."

Keelia stood up, straightened her dress, and tried to pretend that she hadn't just been behaving like a child.

"Shut up," she heard Jericho say as she left.

"I didn't say a word," said Phaedra.

The previous evening had been full of plans. And drinking. And tiny moments of finding reasons to brush up against Jericho. She'd suspected that he was good looking under the beard, but she had been totally unprepared for the heart-stopping good looks that had emerged. Her crush was back and worse than ever. She felt so hamstrung by not being able to talk. She was used to being clever and witty and engaging. How was she supposed to get anywhere when she couldn't even say his name? Probably not by hitting him with a pillow. She'd just thought that if one of her brothers had been hungover, she would have hit them. She hadn't quite counted on him fighting back or that she would like it so much.

She got to the lab and turned on Crystal. They really had made progress between the drinking and Pavel's misguided attempts at dancing. She had work to do.

Phaedra's diagrams were less clear this morning than they had been last night, but Keelia was still able to access the droid database and make the changes to a few significant sub-routines. There had been a good deal of debate over just which sub-routines to change. They needed to give the Board representative—who Jericho said was a fair-minded woman named Thanh Vien—enough evidence that she could legally have Fang arrested and, more importantly, fired. Sadiki said that firing would most likely negate all contracts. It was their hope that with the contracts voided they could take out Fang. Jericho said that Thanh would most likely have armed guards with her, but even without them, he was confident that he could kill Fang. Since Keelia was effectively mute, and the rest of them were contractually bound not to speak out, they couldn't verbally tell Thanh what the problem was. That meant that they needed to present evidence without actually doing anything. That meant droids. It was Keelia's job, with Phaedra's instructions, to have the droids compile security footage into a file that could be presented to Thanh.

An hour later, Keelia destroyed Phaedra's napkin notes and left the droids to do their work. Then, she returned to the job that she was supposed to be doing.

After last night's story about the Soul Sucker artifact, she was even more concerned about the box in the clean room. Keelia had added another few pieces of the artifact the previous week, and now the artifact seemed to be gluing itself back together every time a new piece was added. Two walls were now complete. The magnetism in the room was getting stronger and she'd had to put lids on the sample cases to keep the pieces from moving closer to the box. The previous day, when she'd removed one of the sample lids, she'd found that several pieces in the box had reassembled themselves. She hadn't been able to explain her concerns to the others. For them, it was not an immediate threat.

But after ordering some parts brought up from Fang's workshop, she thought she'd be able to test the magnetic field within the room. Assuming, of course, that the computer would recognize it. It took her most of the afternoon, but she finally made the computer do what she wanted. The results were… not good.

Keelia stared at the screen and tapped her lip. She was so deep in thought that she almost missed Crystal's warning about the lift. She scrambled a bit to make sure that anything incriminating was tucked away and had just returned to the equations board when Fang swept in. She was surprised to see Jericho right behind her. He had the uncomfortable expression that said his nanites were active.

"Good, you're here," said Fang. As if Keelia could be anywhere else. As usual she scanned Keelia's board. Keelia hated it when she pointed out errors. This time her eyes narrowed. "That makes me dizzy. I don't know why you keep working on it."

Keelia pointed into the clean room, by way of explanation. "Yes, never mind about that. It's great progress. I'm sure he'll be very happy."

Keelia's eyes flicked to Jericho, trying to look for a clue as to who the *he* in that sentence was. He also looked nervous. "I've had a thought about the prototype," said Fang. "I realized why you don't want to tell me. You think I'm going to steal your intellectual property."

Keelia opened her mouth to protest.

"And that's totally reasonable. It's not like I'm not willing to give you some credit. So I'm going to have a lawyer droid draw up some papers. Just a little contract to make sure that you get a cut when the gun goes into production. Once you have a contract, then we can all be comfortable and you can tell me about the differential."

Keelia reluctantly nodded. What else was she supposed to do?

"Oh, see! I knew you could be reasonable. I was just coming at it all wrong. But here's the thing. I need you to keep Jericho here."

What?

The word made no sound, but she could see that it came across clearly.

"He and Sadiki always try to slip in some clever language that's to their advantage. He thinks I don't notice, but I do. I won't even let Sadiki know where I am about to be. I made Pavel keep him downstairs. But Jericho is sneaky. And then I remembered!" Fang clapped her hands. "Last time went so well. I'll just do it again."

"Do what?" demanded Jericho.

"Jericho put your arms around Keelia."

Jericho stepped forward and did as he was told. "All right," said Fang patting their shoulders. "That's good. I'll be back to get you in an hour or so. Keelia, you feel free to hurt him all you want. I do. It's fun."

Keelia felt her body go rigid with fury. Fang slid out of the room, humming slightly, unaware of the silent howl of rage that Keelia made behind her back.

"Don't," said Jericho when Keelia spun in his arms and would have gone after her. "It doesn't do any good."

She gestured in fury at the door. It wasn't even sign, it was just anger.

"I know," he said, his breath warm on the back of her neck.

She mimed a punch and a kick.

"Yes, believe me, I know."

She sagged back against him and sighed in frustration. As if acting independently, her head tilted to rest against the side of his face. He adjusted his hold slightly. His nanites seemed to take Fang's orders literally. He couldn't simply put his hands together—his wrists seemed forced to meet. She hoped it wasn't terribly uncomfortable for him, because she liked it.

"You can't sign whatever contract she comes up with," he said quietly.

Keelia agreed, shaking her head, then realized that the head gesture might be unclear. She reached for a tablet on the counter, trying not to move so much that he would have to adjust again.

"I think when she comes back you should tell her how to make the weapon work." Keelia whirled around and faced him furiously, smacking him the arm with the tablet.

"A minute ago you were mad at Fang for suggesting you hurt me."

She smacked him again and his eyes twinkled.

"I talked to Bruges. I get it. Or at least I think I get it. You can't turn on the drill." She nodded emphatically. "But you have to know how the drill works."

She made a *sort of* hand gesture, and began to type on the tablet.

"You could figure it out. And I think you should."

No! The gun targets specific genetic samples. She has me as a sample and when my family comes to get me they'll be easy prey!

"If your family comes—" he began and she stomped her foot.

They will come.

"Keelia, it's been over four months. You're probably right. They probably are looking for you, but we can't know when they'll get here."

You don't believe they're coming?

He hesitated. "No, I don't. Not really. But I stopped believing in a lot of things a long time ago. Water. Sky. Soap. I want to believe. Theoretically, they're possible. But I can't pin everyone's lives on that. I—we—have to do whatever we can to get ourselves out."

Keelia felt tears well up in her eyes.

Whatever it takes.

She dropped the tablet and clunked her forehead into his shoulder with a ragged breath.

"If our plan is to work, we need you to stay free of any contracts and base commands. If you tell her how to make the weapon work, then she'll forget about the contract and she won't hurt you," he said, adjusting his hold again. This time it didn't feel like discomfort—it felt like he was snuggling her. "Maybe you'll even be able to say my name." The last part sounded so wistful that she looked up at him.

Impulse control had always been a problem for her. On the other hand, he obviously wasn't taking a hint. Somebody had to do something.

She leaned up and kissed him.

He pulled back and she blinked up at him, dizzy. For a second, she thought he might say something and then he simply kissed her again. This time she was slightly more prepared. She slid her hand around his neck.

The next time he pulled back, he jerked his hands angrily. "Damn it! I can't touch you. You're right here and I can't," he jerked again, "put a hand on you."

She laughed silently and took advantage of his impairment and distraction to kiss along his neck, sliding her other hand under his shirt. He groaned. It was possible that she was now rating higher than soap.

"Don't they get that I wouldn't actually let you go? I just want—" He silenced himself by kissing her again.

Behind him, Crystal began to flicker and a cascade of beeps erupted from her equipment. Then the whole base shook with an explosion.

His arms abruptly came free and he stumbled back, catching

himself on Crystal's console. He stared at his hands and then at her.

"The mine," he gasped, then sprinted for the door.

She ran after him, but was stopped at the door by her guard droids, who were whirring nervously.

"Priority emergency," was all he said as the lift doors closed.

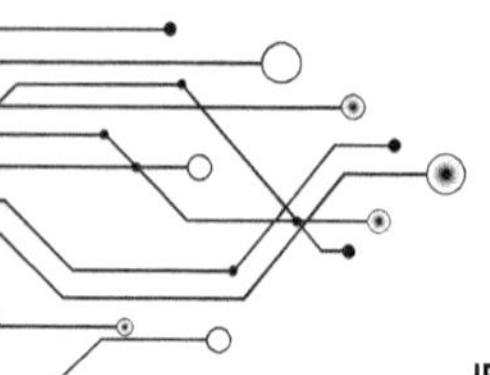

Chapter 18

JERICHO AND THE PRIORITY EMERGENCY

Smoke was pouring out of the mine when Jericho got there. He pulled on a breather mask and fire suit and plunged in. The mine was dim at the best of times, but now even the weak blue Moliter crystal lights had shut down. He scanned the passageway with his head lamp and went to the control panel. There were four life signs up ahead, but they weren't moving. He assigned all available mine units to converge on the location. The scanner was showing a fracture on passage eight, cracks in twelve and six, and a complete collapse in shaft two. This was a problem because shaft two ran parallel to the base water tank. The base tank was designed for the daily needs of two hundred people over the span of a year, with reserves in case space ice could not be located. A crack there and the entire mine could be flooded.

The mine belched in a billow of smoke and dust as he ran down the shaft. Somewhere ahead of him was fire.

He finally found them at the edge of the shaft collapse. Pavel was pinned in place under a mountain of rock. Phaedra and a half-damaged droid were shoveling rock off of him, while above them, on a slipping pile of shale, Bruges and Sadiki tried desperately to seal an ever-growing crack in the water tank—the water tank that, according to the specs, should have had a hundred-year life span and enough resilience to withstand a direct missile strike.

Water was spraying out at every angle.

Sadiki was right—this place was going to fall down around their ears.

"Where is the fire?" he yelled, grabbing Phaedra.

"Other side of the collapse," she yelled back. She shook his hand off and went back to shoveling. "Help Bruges or we'll all drown!"

Jericho ditched the fire suit and scrambled up the sliding hill of rock until he got to Sadiki and Bruges.

"We're losing it!" Sadiki yelled over the rush of water. "The crack needs to be sealed from the inside."

"Bruges!" Jericho grabbed one of the tentacles. "You can go into the tank!"

"Not leaving," said Bruges, slapping on another patch on with his tentacles.

"Go into the tank! You'll be faster. You don't need the air. I'll take your place here!"

Bruges hesitated and then seized the head lamp from Jericho's head and swung off up the passageway, running at top Octoparian speed and using his tentacles to periodically swing from the ceiling.

Jericho was hit in the face with a jet of water. He slapped a seal over it and pushed the sealant gun up to the crack. There was a rumble from the other side of the collapse, and the pile shifted. He could see the bobbing lights of the droids converging on them. Hopefully, that would free Phaedra to help. He didn't have enough arms to truly replace Bruges. He glanced down at Phaedra and Pavel. Pavel was still unconscious and the water was beginning to fill up the divot he was in. Phaedra was making progress, but he wasn't sure if she was going to be fast enough.

He put another seal on and ran the sealant.

"We're going to run out of sealant!" yelled Sadiki, over the sound of the water.

"The droids are coming!" Jericho yelled back and pointed.

"They won't be able to make it up the pile!"

"Take it from them!"

Sadiki nodded and slid down the pile, sitting down and letting gravity carry him at a speed faster than his feet would have been capable of.

Jericho slapped on another seal, and almost had the crack sealed when the sealant gun ran out. He looked back at Sadiki, who was halfway back up the hill and carrying two more sealant guns. Jericho yelled and gestured. Sadiki threw the gun and it landed a few feet from Jericho dove for it as it threatened to slide back down the hill. Fighting for footing, he clambered back up to the crack and ran a line of sealant. There was an ominous creak above him, and he saw a split run down from the ceiling.

Jericho cursed and looked back down at Phaedra. The extra droids had made the difference and she was flinging rock off Pavel's legs by hand now. One of the droids was lowering its load ramp by Pavel's head. Phaedra would have him out soon.

Jericho filled another crack and then was hit in the ribcage by another gout of water. New fractures were streaking out from already sealed cracks in jagged lightning shapes.

"She's loading him!" yelled Sadiki, forcing a patch into place. "How long do we wait?"

Jericho checked the ceiling. The crack was still there, but it hadn't moved. If the tank blew now, it would take them a month to pump out the shaft and repair the tank. Fang would be furious. There was another creak and the crack splintered another few feet down the rock wall.

On the other hand, they would be alive.

"Run," said Jericho.

A year later, after the girl had brought her first child into the world, the Queen took it away from her while she was asleep, and smeared her mouth with blood. Then she went to the King and accused the girl of being a cannibal. The King could not believe this and would not allow anyone to harm her. She, however, sat the whole time sewing on the shirts, and caring for nothing else.

Jacob and Wilhelm Grimm, The Six Swans

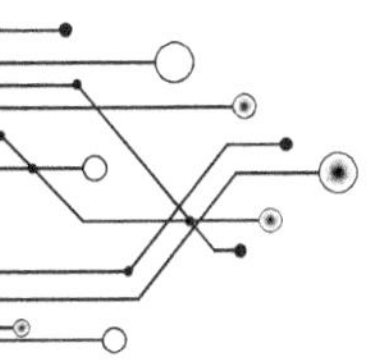

Chapter 19

KEELIA MAKES CHOICES

Keelia lay on her bed in the dark and concentrated on breathing evenly. Every time she thought about something other than breathing, her heart would race, and her breath would come in ragged gasps as if she were running. She was alone in the cell block, and for the first time there were no sounds that weren't hers. No rustles, no soft susurration of air moving in and out of the lungs of five living people, nothing but the frightened pounding of her own heart.

Neither Fang or Jericho had returned to the lab, but the droids had escorted her back to the cell block at the usual time. She could tell that the droids were upset and their normal loops were disrupted. But none of them had communicated anything to her.

Keelia leaped up as she heard the sound of the door opening. The floor lights came on at half-power. Keelia felt her knees go rubbery with relief as Jericho, Phaedra, and Bruges came through the door. They were filthy, caked in the hard silica clay created by water and mine dust. She looked past them, waiting for Pavel and Sadiki, but the door closed.

She hit the wall with her open palm, making them look at her, sparks shooting out from the impact point.

Pavel, Sadiki?

"Med-bay," said Bruges and this time, Keelia really did sit

down on the bed, her hands clutching each other tightly, too scared to sign.

"They're going to be all right," said Jericho, leaning against the solid wall next to her cell. He looked like he needed the wall to stay up right.

"We hope," said Phaedra, leaning against him. He put his arm around her and Keelia felt an ache of jealousy that they could touch and she couldn't reach either of them. Instead, she signed to Bruges that he should do it. He instantly agreed, enveloping them in a multi-tentacle hug. Octoparians were an extremely touch oriented people. They had a hard time with other peoples' boundaries and an even harder time telling when they should and shouldn't hug. Bruges was more than happy to have a hugging moment.

What happened?

"We don't know," said Jericho. "The mine was stable, but something… I don't know, maybe the new orbit? Something caused a pressure detonation in some of the dwarf star alloy at the deepest part of the mine. It caused a collapse in the second shaft next to the water tank. We got it sealed eventually, but we lost a lot of water. And the mine will have to be pumped out and re-drilled."

No. Don't go back in there.

"We don't have a choice," said Jericho tiredly.

No, you don't understand. I don't think it was the new orbit.

"Not the new orbit?" repeated Bruges.

The door slid open and Kodor entered. It was the first time

Keelia had seen him in weeks and she was surprised to see that he looked fatter, as if he'd been doing nothing but eating.

"Why are you all talking?" hissed Kodor. "In cells."

"We're going to take showers," said Jericho tiredly.

"No, mistress say get in cells."

Keelia could see that Jericho didn't want to comply. She could also see that they were all feeling compelled. Kodor waited until they were in and then he approached her cell.

"Mistress also say you come with me," said Kodor. Jericho whirled around, leaping back toward them, but the cell walls snapped into place and he was thrown to the floor with a sharp crack and sizzle of the force field.

Kodor pulled her through the passageways and levels to Fang's lab. Fang was not wearing her apron this time, but she was staring at the weapon. She looked up as Keelia approached.

"There has been a collapse in the mine," she said. "But I'm sure you already know that."

Keelia nodded.

"He's very upset," said Fang. "Very. Upset." The dress made an angry chittering noise. "We were close and now it will take a month to simply clean up the mess. Your mess." Keelia's eyes widened. How was the mine her fault? "You should have been done with the box by now. We would have more control if you were done."

Keelia opened her mouth and no sound came out. The nanites still would not let her speak. She could feel them crawling under her skin.

"I don't know what we're going to do," said Fang. "I've been letting Jericho handle things, but this is… we can't have this. And Jericho is too soft on the others. Maybe I should put Kodor in charge."

Keelia felt herself begin to sweat.

"On the other hand, maybe I should just kill all of them and use the droids. It's not like they're going to live long after we get it done anyway."

Keelia swallowed hard.

"I'll help you with the gun," she said, her voice coming out in a croak. The nanites were still, she liked to think it was out of surprise.

Fang didn't appear to notice the capitulation. "You have to finish the box. He wants you to finish it. And he gets what he wants, doesn't he?"

"I don't think we should finish the box," said Keelia.

"Well, it's not like we have much a choice, now is it?" said Fang, focusing on her directly for the first time.

"What about the Board?" asked Keelia and Fang threw up her hands in frustration. "The mine is going to take a month to pump out and restabilize," said Keelia. "If we worked on the gun, we could finish it by then. And that's when the Board representative is coming, right?"

Fang nodded reluctantly.

"And then I could go back to work on the box." Fang looked tempted. "But you need Jericho and the others. Otherwise the Board representative will be suspicious."

"That's true," admitted Fang. "They like him better. They've always liked him better. I was never fancy enough for them."

"They probably don't like you because you're smarter than they are," said Keelia. "It makes them uncomfortable."

"It really does," said Fang. The dress was swaying as if blown by a breeze. "All right. This is workable. We can do this. He has to wait for the mine anyway. It's his own fault for getting impatient. It's not my fault. So we'll do what we need to do for the Board and then we'll focus on him."

Keelia was starting to worry about *him*.

"You'll stay here and work on the gun, and the others will work on the mine and getting ready for the Board representative. And everything will be just fine." Fang clapped her hands together as if she were announcing tea time.

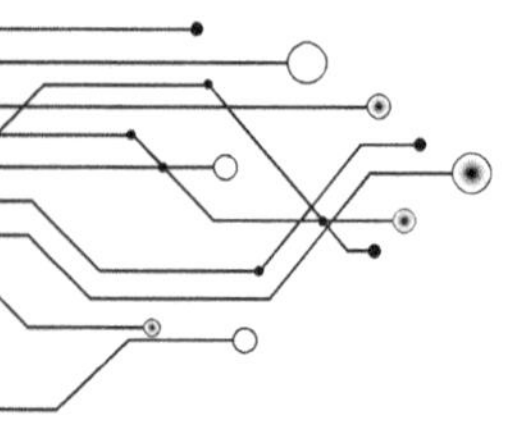

Chapter 20

JERICHO PAYS FANG A VISIT

It took him three days to figure out where Fang was keeping Keelia and another week to find a reason to go up to the workshop.

As he approached, he watched as Fang dropped a tool down from a high shelf onto Keelia's head. Keelia dodged, but just barely. Her medical gown was filthy and her braids were in disarray.

"Fang!" snapped Jericho, and Keelia whirled, opening her mouth.

"No talking, Keelia," said Fang. "We mustn't distract Jericho from his important work with your chitter-chatter. In fact, I don't think you need to move right now at all." Fang patted the now frozen Keelia on the cheek. "How goes the mine rebuild, Jericho? I'm sure you're here to report progress."

"There's progress," said Jericho, trying to look around Fang to Keelia. "But I was hoping to borrow the engineer." He had found that calling Keelia by her name seemed to make Fang angry. He'd switched to using *the engineer*, which seemed to help a bit.

"No, I need her. She's constructing my weapon."

"I thought you just needed her to give access," said Jericho. "Shouldn't you send her back—"

"No, no, no, no," said Fang. "I know you want her for the artifact. But we've discussed this. We have to deal with the immediate problem of the Board. That has to come first."

"Surely the droids could do the work."

"Where would be the fun in that?" demanded Fang. "Besides they're slow and stupid. And they keep dying. Why don't you keep them in better repair?"

"There's wide-spread system decay," said Jericho. "There needs to be a complete overhaul. We've talked about this." He realized he was getting pulled off-mission.

"Overhaul, repairs," muttered Fang, mocking him. "That's all I ever hear from you."

Jericho tried again. "Sorry. Forget about it. I'll work on the droids. But I need the engineer in the mine. There's a complex shoring problem—"

"Oh, you don't want Keelia," said Fang, her eyes narrowing. Jericho sensed that Fang's temper was fraying. "Not down in the mine. It was her fault to begin with."

"What?" Jericho's eyes flicked to Keelia, startled. That wasn't the direction he'd expected Fang to go.

"The selfish girl set off the explosion," said Fang. "That's why I'm keeping her here, away from you. She started experimenting with some of the dwarf star alloy. She thought she could use it to escape."

"No," said Jericho.

"Yes, it's true," said Fang, sadly. "I know you like to think of all of them as your special friends, but honestly, Jericho, when are you going to learn that they don't really care about you?"

Jericho looked at Keelia. She was staring mutely back at him, unable to move. She had been trying to tell them something before Kodor took her away, but it would never have been that. She couldn't possibly have set off an explosion in the mines. Except that they had shown her how to access the droids. Theoretically, it was possible that she could have done it.

He looked at Fang, who smiled at him sweetly. Now he knew it wasn't true.

"I'll handle the problem," he said. "You're right. We probably don't want her in the mine." Fang nodded, oozing smugness. "But we're going to need her for the party with the Board representative. We'll need all of the crew."

Fang looked less pleased. "I'm not really sure—"

"We need the extra girl," said Jericho. "Thanh doesn't really like men too much. We look unbalanced without the engineer."

"I don't think we need any of them," said Fang dismissively.

"We will look odd without them," said Jericho, trying to sound firm. "We need everything to look normal, right?"

Fang swayed slightly as if blown by an invisible breeze, then she made an almost mechanical click sound of displeasure. "Yes, fine. You can have them for the party, but remember that they're not really on your side."

"I'm fully aware of who is on my side," said Jericho.

Two days later, a kitchen droid delivered unsolicited sandwiches to the mine. Wrapped in every sandwich was a note from Keelia. The droids had compiled the file. Delivery was the only remaining obstacle. He didn't show the others, but his note also had the word *kiss* on it. He tucked it in the pocket over his heart.

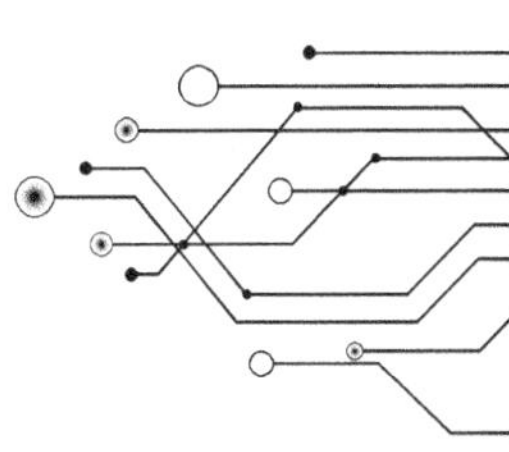

Chapter 21

NIALL'S NEW ARM

Sólveig made another adjustment and Niall's new metal hand twitched.

"Ow!"

"Sorry, but that's good," said Sólveig from behind him as she worked on the arm. He could see the engineer's fluffy blonde-to-white hair bouncing behind his shoulder in the mirror across the room. Tara continued to pace, flipping his knife from hand to hand. He was learning that she didn't sit still well. The knife flipped in another arc, followed by the occasional thump as she dropped it. She also didn't know the first thing about knives. She had been envious of his tricks. He suspected that her lack of skill would not last too much longer.

"Tara!" snapped Sólveig at the next thump. "The floor can't take that kind of abuse."

"It's fine," said Tara. "That one was the ceiling."

"Don't you have some place else to be?" demanded Sólveig.

"No," said Tara, "I'm done working on the *Shard* and now I'm loitering so I can ogle Niall without his shirt on." Niall grinned. He had to admit that having someone to ogle him made the transition to single arm status less painful.

Niall and his father had been at Sólveig's house on a base at the edge of Ránfuglar space for the better part of a month. When he'd woken up in the med-tube aboard the transport freighter, he had been surprised that Tara was still with them. He had thought that she would have been off with the rest of the family, searching for Fang Nazari. When he'd asked her about it, she'd shrugged.

"I have a ship at home," she said. "We'll get your arm fixed up and I'll collect it. Then we can catch up."

A ship had been an understatement. Tara's ship, the *Shard*, looked fast just floating in dry-dock, but he got the sense that Sólveig was annoyed to be returning it to Tara. And even more annoyed that Tara immediately began a system tear-down and overhaul. Tara returned most days covered in engine grease and carrying another modified part that she returned to Sólveig's work desk with a meaningful thump. Tara did not appreciate the changes Sólveig had made to the *Shard* in her absence.

Meanwhile, Niall's father was enjoying visiting someone else's workshop, but Niall could tell Langston was starting to chafe at being without his family and, perhaps equally importantly, his own workshop. Niall was sympathetic and he was certainly anxious to get to his sister, but Tara was making waiting a lot easier.

He wasn't sure his father had noticed that Niall and Tara were no longer sleeping in separate rooms and he was wondering if he should bring it up. Langston was notoriously oblivious to these things and the family usually relied on their mother to point them out. Niall didn't think his father would care, but it might prevent awkwardness later. Sólveig, of course, had noticed right away and had not approved.

"Ow," he said again and Sólveig made another adjustment.

"Almost there," she muttered.

"Uplink is coming online," yelled Langston from the next room.

"Sólveig," said Niall, attempting to stand up.

"Almost there," she said.

He began to inch away from the bench. "Ow!"

"Hold still and it would hurt less!" she snapped.

"My family," he said, pointing toward the next room.

"Fine," she said, putting the tuning tool down. "I'm done. Don't come complaining to me when your thumb won't straighten."

"I'll be right back," he said.

"Uh-huh," Sólveig grunted.

He hurried from the room, grabbing his shirt as he went. The link was live when he reached the office. He could see the real-time rendering of the *Black Tree*, the family's main ship.

"Oh, how is that fair?" demanded Anwell, gesturing to Niall's new arm as he entered. "You're not even going to have to work out now."

Niall looked down at his metal arm, and rapidly pulled his shirt on.

"Anwell!" snapped Rayna.

"Did you find her?" demanded Langston, ignoring their son's commentary.

"Did you?" seconded Niall.

Anwell and Rayna exchanged looks and Niall felt his shoulders sag, which was a thing worth marveling at because up until two days ago he'd only had one shoulder to drop. But it didn't change the fact that Keelia was still missing.

"She wasn't on the asteroid?" asked Niall.

"No asteroid," said Anwell.

"What?" Niall and Langston looked at each other in shared confusion. "How is that possible?" demanded Niall.

"Remember how big that exhaust shaft was? Matty and I think it was because the asteroid itself was mechanized. Mat's out in a scout ship now. He's got some sort of theory about an ion gas trail."

"Yes!" exclaimed Langston. "Tell him to send me the signature. Keelia and I talked about that one time."

"Sending it now," said Rayna, smiling at her husband.

"Can you follow it?" asked Niall.

"Mat thinks so," said Anwell. "It seems pretty dissipated though. I'm not sure how easy that's going to be."

"It's about three months old," said Langston looking at his tablet. "I'll send a scrub and scan program that will make it easier."

"Three months," said Niall taking a nervous breath. "So she was alive three months ago."

"Alive and hacking systems," said Langston proudly.

"That's our girl," said Rayna. "How soon can you rejoin us?" She asked, scrutinizing Niall and his new arm.

"We can leave in three days," said Tara from the doorway. "Niall needs a bit more fine tuning to be completely functional. But I have a fast ship. I've plotted the jump gates already. We can catch up to you in two weeks."

"That's good," said Rayna, taking in Tara and Niall's knife still dangling from her hand. Niall guessed that in that brief scrutiny his mother had concluded exactly where he was sleeping. "I don't think we've ever discussed your interest in this asteroid, Ms. Carbanado," said his mother.

"I have zero interest in the asteroid," said Tara. "I want to kill Fang Nazari."

"And I, for one, am one-hundred percent supportive of that goal," said Anwell.

"As are we all," said Rayna drily. "But I think I'd like to know why."

Tara glanced at Niall, and he nodded. He'd already covered this ground with her. There was no reason the rest of the family couldn't know. He just got the feeling that she wasn't used to having all of her cards on the table.

"Two years ago, I received a message from a friend of mine. It wasn't intended to go to me. He was, I think, attempting to reroute a distress call through the mail system."

"Two years?" asked Rayna.

"I was… otherwise occupied at the time and it took me a year to figure out what, or rather, *who* had done this."

She tapped a few buttons on her com bracelet and the display split, showing the video from her archives.

The inside of an Octoparian ship appeared, water sluicing out of cracked wall pods. The light from Moliter white crystals were flickering. The image swung wildly, interspersed with static.

"This treaty violation," gasped a voice. There was an electric sizzle and a tentacle flopped into the field of view. Then the image swung again, the camera probably being held by another tentacle, and a tall form appeared on the screen. Her hair was turquoise and she carried a spear in one hand and the trailing ends of a tazer net.

Behind her, a man with black hair stood, appearing to strain against nothing.

"We need him," the man yelled.

"You need him," replied Fang Nazari. "I don't need anyone." She hefted the spear in one hand and then the image cut out entirely.

"My friend is—was, an Octoparian named Bruges," said Tara. "He was on a mission to find a new home ocean for his family. In case you've never met an Octoparian, they're pacifists who like to hug a lot and *she* had him wrapped in an electric net."

"I recognize the man in the video," said Anwell. "He was there when we were captured. Who is he?"

"Actually, he was the one that helped me figure out who she was," said Tara. She pulled up a still image of the man. Then zoomed in on his shirt where a Nazari Corporation logo could almost be seen. "Once I knew to look at the Nazari Corp. I was able to hire a hacker to do some digging." She flicked her hand and a military ID shot slid in to replace the previous image.

"Jericho Nazari," read Anwell. "Are we sure that's the same guy?"

"Facial recognition says it is," said Tara. "And he led me to his father, Marid." she showed another image of a man with a beard.

"I guess there's a family resemblance," said Rayna. "The beard makes it stronger. What about the woman?"

"Marid's wife. Jericho's step-mother." Tara flicked her hand again and an image of a pretty woman with black hair appeared. "Fang Nazari."

They all stared at the image.

"That's barely…" began Anwell, and then shook his head. "What happened to her?"

"Modification of some kind," said Tara with a shrug. "Marid is dead. Jericho took leave from the military to escort his father's body home and never returned."

"Go back to the son's profile," ordered Rayna. Tara did as she was asked and they all read Jericho Nazari's service record.

"He's got to be helping her," said Langston. "Otherwise, how could someone keep a Blue Band on a moon base?"

"I don't know," said Anwell. "He didn't want her to kill the Octoparian. And he wasn't fighting for her when we were there."

"He didn't try to stop her," argued Tara.

"Yeah, but if I had a guy like that on my side I wouldn't let the manigator lead the troops." Anwell was not to be persuaded.

"Well, when we find him, we will ask him," said Rayna, and the tone in her voice suggested that all questions would be answered one way or another.

"Manigator?" repeated Niall skeptically.

"Crocoman?" tried Anwell.

"Manodile?" suggested Langston.

Rayna sighed heavily and looked at Tara, who visibly repressed a laugh. "Returning to the topic at hand. Niall's arm will be… fully functional in three days?"

"If Sólveig is right, then yes, the neural relay synchronization should be done by then," said Langston, pulling up a diagram of the new metal spider web that now ran from Niall's arm to his brain. "It's really fascinating."

Rayna closed her eyes briefly and Niall got the feeling that she did not share Langston's enthusiasm. Then she opened her eyes and smiled. "I'm sure that it is. You'll send us your jump route?" she asked, focusing on Tara, who nodded.

"Good, then we can keep searching, and not wait."

"We'll see you soon," said Langston. "I love you all."

"We love you too," said Rayna.

Later that night, Niall was lying in bed watching his fingers move. Tara was standing by the window watching the planet set.

"It's slow to react," he said.

"Sólveig will tune that up," she said. "You have to be patient while your brain adjusts to the new wiring."

"Does she not like me?" he asked. Tara looked back at him, surprised. "She really seems to disapprove of us."

"Oh," said Tara. "No. She disapproves of me. She thinks you're too good for me."

Niall ran that through his brain a few times. "No, that still doesn't make sense. Try again."

"You may not have noticed this, but I'm a bit of a scoundrel. A ruffian. In general, not a very nice person."

"You're nice to me," he said.

"I like you."

"You've been nice to my family."

"I like them too. Your brothers are funny and your dad is sweet. Your mom is a little scary—I'm not going to lie. But that kind of just makes me like her too."

Niall smiled, but shook his head. "I still don't understand."

"Bruges, the Octoparian, he didn't understand either," she said with a smile. "I met him on Eras 8. Like I said, he was looking for a new ocean. He was looking for a local pilot who knew the jump points and could get him around without coming against pirates and raiders."

"And you took the job?"

"Yeah, I did. But the reason I could get past the pirates was because I knew most of them. Hell, I've crewed with half of them. I've done some smuggling. I robbed a bank once. Not a big one, and I sent the money back eventually, but I did it. I'm too smart for boring jobs and too stupid not to get caught doing the fun ones. My family gave up on me a long time ago. Bruges, on the other hand, said giving up on your friends was not acceptable. That stupid alien trusted people. He trusted me." Her voice cracked and she looked away. "I should have been there for him. And I am not going to let that… woman get away with killing him."

Niall got up and joined her at the window. He liked that she was almost his height. It made kissing her that much easier.

He used one finger to pull her face toward him and cocked his head until she couldn't avoid eye contact. "We will get Keelia back and we will kill Fang Nazari. I promise. Even if we have to blow up that damn asteroid to make it happen, I swear it will be done."

A reluctant smile slid across her lips. "You say the sweetest things."

"You just like blowing things up," he said after he had demonstrated their height-to-kissing properties. She shrugged her agreement. "Although, while we're on the topic. I do think you've been spending too much time with the wrong people."

"Now you sound like Sólveig," she said, sourly.

"Yeah, she's one of the ones you need to stop spending time with. I mean, sure, she's nice enough, and obviously great at her job. I'm more than happy to send more work her way and we can come back for holidays and whatever, but… come on. If your family won't at least try to come get you out of a Rantarian Slave Mart, do they even deserve to be called family?"

She stared at him a long moment. "Go get on the bed," she ordered.

"Why?" he asked, grinning hopefully.

"Because I'm about to do very bad things to you and I don't want to short out your arm."

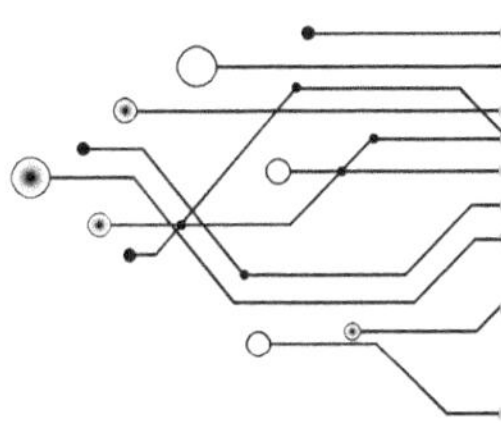

 Chapter 22

KEELIA PREPARES FOR THE PARTY

Keelia watched as Fang fired the gun at the small herd of cloned sheep running down the main decking, clustering together in wild terror. As the beam from the gun caught swept over the herd, one sheep, and only one of the sheep, screamed . Seconds later there was nothing left but a pile of goop.

"Beautiful," said Fang with a sigh.

"There seem to be fewer sheep than last week," observed Keelia.

"Population control," growled Kodor.

Keelia didn't point out that the sheep couldn't breed. She simply glanced down at Kodor's sleekly plump belly. Once Fang had given him control of the clone unit, there had been no stopping him. The cleaner mechanicals were working overtime on the main promenade, which is where he ran his hunting gallery.

Fang adjusted a few more dials and then liquidated the entire herd. "Excellent!" she said with a cackle. "This will be just the thing!"

Keelia wished she could feel pleased or angry or something about what she'd just seen. But the truth was that she just felt numb. She was too tired to care anymore. She'd spent the past month in Fang's office, sleeping on a pile of old chair cushions under a desk and dodging the tools that Fang routinely flung at her. She hadn't always succeeded. Fang locked her into a tiny supply closet at night and had to be reminded to let her use the bathroom. Food had been intermittent, as had Fang's sanity. She'd once spent an entire day hiding in a cramped tool cabinet as Fang had raged outside. She now had a very clear understanding about how Jericho felt about soap. She tried periodically to clean herself up, but the workroom sink was tiny and Fang always seemed meaner after she was clean.

The lift door opened and there was a small cough.

"I'm busy," said Fang without turning around.

"It's time to prepare for the party," said Phaedra. "We require the engineer."

Keelia had noticed that Jericho and the others, in the occasional brief glimpses she'd had of them, had taken to referring to her as *the engineer*. It did seem to keep Fang in a calm state of mind, but Keelia found it disheartening.

"Oh," said Fang, looking around and spotting Keelia. "Yes. I'm done with her. Keelia, be a *lamb* and go with her."

Keelia glanced at the puddles of goop on the floor and back at Fang, still holding the gun. She nodded and walked to the lift. She kept her back straight and tried not to break into a run. She tried to never show Fang any weakness.

The doors closed and Phaedra hugged her. Keelia leaned into her and tried not to cry, but wasn't very successful.

"Oh Keelia," said Phaedra, hugging her tighter. "We got your notes."

Keelia smiled, and stood up, wiping her face. Sending notes via the server droids had kept her from totally losing it.

"I think Jericho keeps all of his under his pillow," said Phaedra. "But the rest of us give them to Pavel and he turns all of them into origami cranes. For the record, we also enjoyed the sandwiches."

Keelia impulsively hugged Phaedra again and, again, tried not to cry. Just having someone talk to her in a normal tone of voice was comforting.

"Still can't talk?"

Keelia shook her head.

"That's fine. We have a plan for that. You're going to be the brilliant engineer who was damaged in an industrial accident. Bruges is your interpreter. In a way, it's good, because otherwise we were going to have a hard time explaining an Octoparian on board."

The lift opened and Keelia looked out in surprise at level one. It was the first time she'd been allowed up to this level. One entire wall was covered in plants. Ornate potted palms marked the entrances to most doors—like all space furniture they were anchored to the floor in case of gravity failure. But all the anchors on this level were ornate gold swirls and flourishes, designed to look as non-functional as possible. The Nazari Corporation logo was picked out in gold on the silver deck plating. And enormous chandeliers made of rock crystal hovered high above, lighting everything with a glimmering warm light. Everything was polished to a gleaming shine, but nothing moved. It was very grand, but Keelia couldn't help comparing it to the *Black Tree* that constantly vibrated with life, movement and color. Keelia looked questioningly at Phaedra.

"It's a party," said Phaedra. "We can't get ready for it in the cell block. There has to be dresses and hair and things. I mean, for you. I'm playing the head of security, so I get a fancy uniform with pants. Which is good, because I'd rather be dead than in a dress."

Keelia raised an eyebrow.

"Well, maybe not really, but I swear it's close."

For the first time in weeks, Keelia laughed. Phaedra smiled back and put her arm around her shoulders. She had the sense that Phaedra was doing her best to be extra light-hearted and encouraging. Which was probably a bad sign for how terrible Keelia looked. "Now, come on. Let's get you a bath and you can pick out a ridiculous hairstyle and a fancy dress."

The bath was everything Keelia had been dreaming of, but Phaedra would not let her crawl straight into the big three-person sized bed in the suite afterward.

"I know. But we don't have time for naps. I wish we did. I'd let you sleep for a week," said Phaedra, pushing her in the direction of the hair-stylist droid. Keelia sighed and picked a hair style at random—it was some sort of half-up, half-down thing that would leave her with a waterfall of hair on one side. It would probably be annoying, but Keelia no longer cared. She let herself drift off in a tiny nap while the droids worked her hair and makeup.

When she woke up, Phaedra was fully dressed in a high-collared black uniform. It looked crisp against her green hair. Keelia clapped her approval.

"Yeah, I know," said Phaedra turning to look in the mirror. "I look good. Also, have you seen my ass in these pants? When we get out of here, I'm getting six more just like these." She flipped up the coat tail to shake her butt at Keelia, who laughed again. "You are looking pretty shiny too. What dress are you going to wear?"

Keelia shrugged. The tables seemed to have turned. Where Phaedra seemed filled with optimism that their escape plan would work, Keelia now only felt a gnawing sense of fear. What was the point of getting dressed? What was the point of any of it?

"Come on, come on. Enough of this *who cares drang skit*. We have to pick out something that will make Jericho's eyes pop." Phaedra pulled Keelia to the closet and pushed her into position to let the wardrobe scan her for sizing. Phaedra waited until the scan was completed and began to flip through the dresses on the display. "No, no, no." The scroll picked up speed.

Keelia abruptly reached out and stopped the carousel of dresses. She went back two and tapped her selection.

"Oh yes," said Phaedra. "You're right. That's the one."

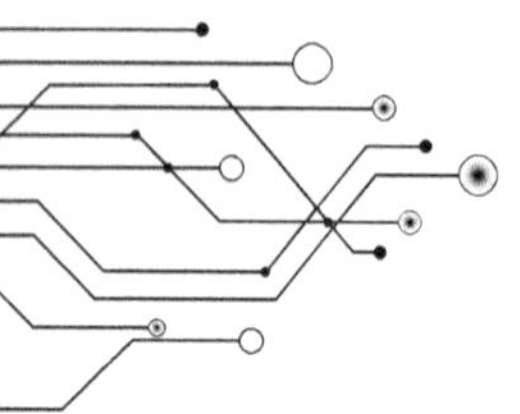

Chapter 23

JERICHO AND THE BATTLE

Jericho waited in the foyer and tried not to touch anything. He was worried about Keelia. He was worried about everything. Thanh's arrival was imminent. All they had to do was pretend everything was normal until Fang took her to see the gun. The safety goggles that Fang would hand her were pre-programmed to show the data file of security footage that Keelia had compiled. It ended in a simple request, that Thanh should tell Fang she was fired.

A simple request that he hoped would free them from any compulsions.

They would be next to the weapons locker at that point. He was certain he could take it from there. And if all else failed, he had a droid pre-programmed to give Fang a shot that contained enough Hydrogen Cyanide to kill six people and an elephant.

He tugged at the collar of his gray suit and wished he hadn't let Sadiki convince him that the suit was necessary. But it was either this or his military uniform and he didn't feel qualified to wear that anymore.

"Hey," said Pavel coming in. Pavel was now officially in the base records as the Head of Mining operations. He had cleaned up and put on a suit, but he still managed to look one beer away from starting a fight. "You seen the girls yet? Phaedra got Keelia, right?"

"Phaedra said it went fine," he said. She had also said that Keelia seemed… worn, but he didn't need to say that to Pavel.

Sadiki came in, straightening his cuffs. He looked, for once, like Jericho remembered him—polished, poised and the picture of elegance. Bruges bustled in right after him. There was nothing to be done with an Octoparian. Dressing up for them was eating extra fish oil, so their tentacles were shiny and full of pucker.

"Well," said Jericho, looking them over. "I guess we look about as good as we're going to."

"Speak for yourself," said Phaedra coming down the stairs. "I don't just look good. I look *fjandinn* hot."

He grinned. She did, but he couldn't stop himself from looking behind her for Keelia.

"She'll be down in a minute," said Phaedra. The others at least pretended not to notice Jericho's crush, but Phaedra called him out every time. "Make her laugh," Phaedra added quietly, drawing closer. "She needs it."

There was a rustle of fabric from the top of the stairs and he looked up. He felt as if all of the air had been knocked out of his lungs. Her hair was down in a tumble over one shoulder and her dress was pale gold in draping satin fabric that swayed as she walked.

"Might want to close your mouth," said Phaedra quietly.

"Bu—" It wasn't so much a statement as an inarticulate primal grunt.

"Oh, I know," said Phaedra. "I saw her put it on. Maybe if tonight goes well, you can see her take it off."

"Don't jinx me," he muttered. Keelia reached the bottom of

the stairs and he found that a childhood of training had not been erased by a mere six years of tortuous imprisonment. He stepped forward and offered her his arm, as if this were truly a ball in his father's house.

She smiled up at him as she took his arm, but her face was serious. She had lost some of her sparkle and he felt a swell of panic.

"We tried to get Bruges in a tux," he said. "But we couldn't figure out where to put the bowtie." She laughed and the twinkle came back.

"You look like the sun and the moon," said Pavel, smiling.

Jericho looked down at his gray suit and her gold dress. He supposed they did.

She lifted her hands and made a quick sign.

"She say: no poetry, Pavel. You lose reputation."

Pavel laughed. "I'm not worried. I know you won't blab."

Keelia stuck her tongue out at him and Jericho tried not to laugh. "All right, that's enough. Time to be serious. Everyone knows the plan? Just stay calm and play it straight. We'll all get through this."

"I think," said Sadiki and then stopped. "Yes," he said, shaking his head, seeming to change his mind about what he'd been about to say. "Let's all get through this."

Keelia took a nervous breath and tucked her hand back into Jericho's arm. He smiled down at her. Perhaps Pavel was right. Perhaps she was the sun and she had pulled him into her orbit and he would spin around her forever.

They walked to the far end of the hall where the grandiose

double doors to the docking bay stood, seeking to impress no one, since no one used them anymore. Fang was waiting for them, surrounded by a contingent of droids. She eyed Jericho and Keelia and he knew he'd made a mistake in taking her arm. He released Keelia and went to stand next to his step-mother. The others stood across from them, awaiting their guests.

Fang was looking more human than she usually did. She was standing at a normal height, without using the dress to loom over anything, and her hair was black again. She had put on some sort of makeup that returned her skin to an almost flesh-like color. Even the dress was being remarkably quiet and barely moved. She was really trying.

"Well, doesn't everyone look nice," said Fang. "Almost like human beings. I mean, except for that one," she said pointing to Bruges. "You look nothing like a human. I wouldn't dream of insulting you that way."

Bruges inclined his head as a way of acknowledging the comment. Which was probably for the best. There was no good way to respond to that. Jericho didn't know about the others, but the façade of humanity felt extremely thin at the moment. Perhaps Bruges was the lucky one—at least he didn't have to pretend. There was a hiss as the doors on the far side of the airlock opened. He could see Thanh Vien in the door way with a retinue of five others.

"Remember, Jericho," said Fang. "We're family. We have to stick together. And I will kill all of them if you even think about leaving me." Then she smiled.

Thanh Vien entered through the double doors in a dress

made of enormous red roses that set off her ivory skin to perfection. Her almond eyes took in the scene, and then she focused on Fang.

"Fang," she purred. "So nice to see you again after all this time."

"Thanh," said Fang, her tone cool. Jericho could tell from that single word that Fang really had no memory of meeting Thanh previously. They embraced and exchanged kisses in the air above their cheeks. Contact was for people who liked each other.

"Jericho," said Thanh, moving to him next. The greeting was the same. Although, perhaps it was his imagination, but he thought that she squeezed his arm a little. "Do you know, I have never been to this base? It was a labor of love for your father—I'm excited to see it."

"It's a moon base," said Fang, dampeningly.

"I'll be happy to show you around after dinner," said Jericho. "But first let me introduce you to our staff. I'm sure you remember our lawyer, Sadiki Kendrick."

"Sadiki, so lovely to see you." Thanh's welcome to him was the first that seemed truly genuine, and Sadiki's smile seemed equally real.

"This is our Director of Mining Operations, Pavel Monro and Phaedra Galanos, the Head of Security." Thanh smiled and bowed slightly in the perfunctory way. "This is Keelia Black, an engineer, and her interpreter, Bruges."

Thanh eyed Keelia. "I met several Blacks during Rautt Uprising," she said. "They were all of the Swan Clan. Are you, by chance, related?"

Keelia inclined her head.

"Keelia," said Fang, her head tilting, inspecting Keelia with new interest. "You never mentioned that your family was in the Chimeran military."

"They weren't," said Thanh. "They were Alliance, but they held the supply line for the rebels."

"The Swan Clan," said Bruges as Keelia signed, "honors all pledges. The Swan and Rautt had agreements. Business is business."

Fang barked a laugh. "Indeed."

Jericho now wanted to ask more questions. The Rautt were one of the few planets to leave the Alliance. Its exit had been a victory for the Chimera Compact, but it was his impression that Keelia's family were pro-Alliance. It was one of the reasons that he didn't really think her family would come—the Alliance didn't operate out here. But if they were already familiar with Chimera space and had allies here, they might actually come looking for her. Not for the first time, he wished that they could talk like normal people.

"I am pleased to meet all of you," said Thanh. "These are my associates…" She went over their names, but Jericho found them dropping out of his head as soon as she said them. They had titles like Secretary and Personal Assistant. Their titles were just as fake as the ones he had given his fellow prisoners. In his mind, the word 'bodyguard' floated over each of their heads. He glanced at Fang to see if she was buying anything that Thanh said and saw her dress twitch and raise her up a little—she was already starting to slip.

"Shall we go into dinner?" asked Jericho. He needed Fang to make it through dinner to the weapons demonstration.

"Yes," said Fang. "That sounds excellent. People always like food."

Something in the way she said it made it sound like she wasn't including herself as *people*, and it occurred to him that he hadn't seen her eat anything other than bits of her dress in a very long time.

"That sounds delightful," said Thanh. "Jericho, I know Fang will be more comfortable on your arm. Perhaps Sadiki could escort me in? It would give us a chance to catch up."

"I would be delighted," said Sadiki, offering Thanh his arm.

Fang watched the procedure as if she was trying to remember how it was done. Jericho held out his arm and she copied Thanh's movements. Once again, he was surprised by how cold she was, even through the sleeve of his jacket.

Dinner was interminable, although Jericho did take a moment to watch Pavel. Pavel neither overindulged or embarrassed them. In fact, he was making entirely appropriate small-talk. It was a small triumph and totally pointless in the greater scheme of things, but Jericho couldn't help feeling a bit of pride. Phaedra, of course, was doing fine. Sadiki was talking to Thanh. It was Keelia who looked bored. Unable to talk easily, no one was talking to her. She caught his eye and he winked. She tried to bury a smile and returned to eating whatever ridiculous chilled microscopic watermelon infused basil molecular shrimp aspic thing that was the middle course. Fang was pushing hers around her plate. He thought she'd taken about two bites of soup as well. The dress was quiet, but he sensed that she was simply biding her time. And in fact, Thanh had barely put down her dessert fork when Fang clapped her hands.

"Let's go kill some sheep!"

"I beg your pardon," said Thanh, looking surprised.

Fang froze. "I'm afraid we've been indulging in some rather tasteless humor about our weapons tests. I blame Keelia. It's what happens when you work with juveniles."

Thanh glanced at Keelia, who neither protested nor acknowledged the sudden attack. Jericho found that he was gripping his dessert fork with a weapon-like intensity and he could tell that at least two of Thanh's associates had noticed. He gently put down the fork.

"It's what happens when we don't have guests," he said. "We'll have to have people in more often to keep us civil."

Fang blinked at him. "We did used to have more people around," she said, looking around the room as if expecting them to appear. As if she hadn't slaughtered the entire kitchen staff in this very room.

"Well, I'm sure people are just waiting for an invitation," said Thanh soothingly. "I'm very excited to see the weapons test."

"Of course," said Fang, nodding. "It's very good. I make very good weapons."

"You always have," agreed Thanh, and Jericho was relieved that she seemed to have picked up on Fang's instability.

Fang led the way down to the weapons gallery. Kodor had shoved seven freshly made sheep out onto the concourse and waited by the weapons locker. Jericho could tell that Thanh was disgusted by Kodor's presence. Floor-up mutant builds weren't illegal in open space, but they were certainly tasteless to introduce into polite society. Jericho had forgotten that—he had simply moved on to hating Kodor.

Fang eagerly picked the weapon up from the table where she had placed it, hefting the large gun without problems.

"Safety first," murmured Jericho and Fang blinked again. "Right. Put on goggles or whatever. No one likes splatter in the eye."

A droid rolled forward and offered Thanh a pair—*the* pair—pre-loaded with the loop of Fang's misdeeds. Thanh slipped them on and Jericho watched as her body jerked in surprise.

Fang was covering the exciting properties of the gun, oblivious to what Thanh was viewing.

"And you see," said Fang, wiping a smear of sheep's blood on the receptor. "Simply place the sample here and you can select an individual or an individual's family. Kodor, if you would."

Kodor smacked his tail and roared. The startled sheep jumped and began to run. Fang leveled the gun and Jericho watched the beam sweep over the herd, but just one dropped, screaming. It was the first time he'd ever seen the gun work. It was terrifying.

He tore his eyes off the puddle that had been a sheep and looked around at the collected group of humans. Pavel and Phaedra had moved closer to Kodor. Sadiki and Keelia remained where they were, giving the semblance of normalcy.

Thanh took off the goggles with a ragged breath. Jericho tensed. "Fang," said Thanh, and Fang turned, smiling at Thanh, the gun still in her arms. "You're fired and I will personally see to it that you're arrested and tried for murder."

Jericho immediately felt a lessening of pressure in his arms. Phaedra and Pavel leaped for Kodor and Jericho launched himself at Fang. He knew he struck true, but suddenly she was no longer there and he was in over his head in a sea of the dress, the bugs, clawing at his mouth and eyes, trying to crawl up his nose and in his ears. A hand reached in and pulled him out.

Sadiki gave another heave and Jericho was free of the dress. But behind him he heard the skittering scrabble of a million tiny legs on the deck plating and then Fang laughed, her high mad cackle.

"Do you think you've won anything?" Fang demanded, hefting the gun and leveling it at them. Thanh's bodyguards were battling droids on their way back to the lift. Kodor and Phaedra were locked in battle and Pavel was bashing in the door to the weapons locker. "Pre-sets are a marvelous thing. Particularly, when your ship uploads me the medical profiles." She pulled the trigger and one of the bodyguards dropped. One more click of the dial, another bodyguard. Thanh was running, but Jericho didn't think she was going to make it.

Jericho grabbed Sadiki by the shoulder. "Get the poison." Then he sprinted to the weapons locker. Together he and Pavel kicked the door open. Suddenly Pavel doubled over, clutching his leg.

"The nanites," Pavel gasped, his eyes wide. "Hurry!"

Jericho didn't wait, he reached into the weapons locker and pulled out his glaive. It came to his hand like an old friend.

He turned back and ran at Fang, lighting up the blade. The dress fountained at him and he sliced the tendrils away. Two more steps and he'd be within reach of Fang's neck. He pulled his arm and she reached out her hand, her face twisted in a snarl.

His arm froze in place. He fought the nanites in his body. He could feel them eating into his nerve endings, the pain screaming down across his chest. He was so close. He took one more step. He could feel the dress wrapping around his legs.

There was a roar and Sadiki tackled Fang, aiming to take her out at the knees. But the dress parted and there was nothing there. No legs. Sadiki sprawled onto the floor and the dress enveloped him. Behind Fang, Bruges seemed to drop out of the ceiling, Keelia in his tentacles. Keelia slid down Bruges arms and onto Fang's back and jabbed Fang with a long needle.

Fang flung Keelia over her shoulder and against the wall. She lifted the gun and fired again as Thanh entered the lift. Thanh screamed and Jericho knew that they were all going to die. He pushed past the pain and took another step.

"One more step, Jericho, and I will break his neck," said Fang, backing up, the dress holding up Sadiki, by his neck. Jericho hesitated.

Sadiki reached up, pushed the plunger on the syringe. Fang—or the dress—snapped his neck.

Jericho heard himself yelling, but it was as if from a long way away. Fang seemed to stagger and then she plucked the syringe out of her neck and dropped it on the floor. The pain was unbearable now, his vision was blurring and narrowing to a tunnel.

"That might have worked," said Fang, sliding closer to him. "If I'd had any functioning organs left."

He pulled his arm with the glaive down in a last desperate attempt and it sliced through the dress like it was smoke. There was nothing underneath. There was only the dress.

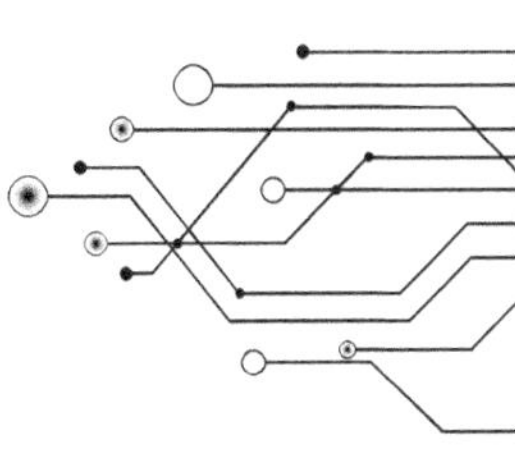

Chapter 24

KEELIA BLACK

Keelia lay on the floor of her cell where the droids had dropped her. Her neck was one long stretch of fire. Her head was still bleeding sluggishly from where she had connected with the wall. From her position, she could see the corner of Bruges cell, where he was bound in one giant bundle of tentacles. She looked at Jericho's cell. It was empty. Because of course it was. Fang had taken him.

Fang had killed Sadiki and taken Jericho.

She stared at her hands, one clenched in a fist, the other open, the nails torn and bleeding from where she'd been drug along the floor.

She remembered, suddenly, her mother returning from a mission, her nails split, covered in blood and tears streaking her face. Niall had been with her and his face had been gray.

How old had she been? Six? Later she'd learned that Uncle Ailill, Declan's father, would not be returning. She'd been fifteen before she asked her mother about it. She'd been horrified at the answer.

How did you keep going, Mum?

I kept going because I loved my family, but mostly because I had to kill the ones who took Ailill from us. That's what it means to be a Black, Keelia. We do whatever it takes to survive. We do whatever it takes to win.

She loved her mother. Rayna was the originator of surprise attack hugs, forts in the living quarters, dessert for breakfast, and secret midnight girls meetings. But Rayna had always been harder, meaner, scarier than Keelia could ever conceive of being. Keelia was not sure that she had the capacity to do what was necessary to survive and win. Whatever was necessary was hard, messy and cost perhaps more than she was willing to give.

Keelia always tried not to let the family down, but she knew that she would never be a warrior like her mother, Niall and Anwell. She wasn't a pilot like Mat, she couldn't heal people like Jed, and she didn't have the gifts that Easton and Graves did. She had never really been like the others. She was too light-hearted, too easily distracted by shiny new knowledge and toys. She was soft. It was one of the reasons she thought she should try for a solid engineering job. Keelia had decided that she should do something where her family wouldn't have to count on her—the least of the Blacks—in a life or death situation.

The lights went out in the cell block. She reached out the open hand and tapped the cell wall twice. Somewhere down the cell block, there was another two flashes. Then another two from the other side of the room.

Pavel and Phaedra were still alive.

Keelia lay on the floor and tried not to sleep, but at some point drifted off in an uneasy slumber full of hellish dreams.

The next morning, the walls dropped, and two droids entered with Kodor right behind them. His arm was in a cast from where Phaedra had broken it. He pointed one of the droids to Bruges.

"You will go with the droids," he hissed at Keelia. "The box will be completed. No more delays. The rest of you will go to the mine," said Kodor as Bruges expanded out of his constraints with a sigh of relief.

"Where is Jericho?" demanded Phaedra.

Kodor hit Pavel with his tail and Pavel bounced off the wall and onto the floor.

"Hey!" yelled Phaedra, in shock.

"The mistress keeps him," said Kodor. "Pray you don't join him."

"You don't understand, we need Jericho in the mine," said Phaedra, picking Pavel up off the floor. Her face was white under the bruises. Pavel wiped blood from his mouth.

"No," said Kodor, his red tongue sliding out from between his teeth and flicking out into Phaedra's face. "*You* give the mistress what *she* needs. She has been too nice to you. No more. Every time one of you does not do as asked, I will hurt other of you. If that does not work I will hurt Jericho. The mine will be completed. The artifact will be completed. You will all submit. There are no other choices."

Phaedra surged forward, but Keelia grabbed her by the arm and Pavel put out his arm blocking her path.

"No other choices," hissed Kodor.

Keelia bowed her head and followed the droids out of the room. Her left hand was still clenched in a fist. She entered the lab and looked around. Everything was just as she'd left it. On the wall, she could see the calendar of days that marked how long she had been here: five months and eight days.

She went through the lab into the supply closet and found a glass container with a lid. Very carefully, she put her fist over it and opened her fingers. A green, iridescent speck the size of a sequin dropped into the beaker and she slammed the lid closed on it.

Going back to the door, Keelia sent one of the droids for a medical gown, stripped out of the tattered remains of her evening gown and scrubbed up in the sink. She tried to think anything coherent while she scrubbed. She felt numb and worn down to dust. She gripped the edge of the sink and stared as the water, grime and blood finished swirling down the drain. The droid returned and handed her a medical gown. She put it on as if by rote. She felt detached as she watched her hands fasten the straps on her shoulders.

Keelia picked up a grease pen and wrote on the wall where Steve's brains had been.

QUICQUID CAPIT.

She knew what she was up against now. She would find Jericho. She would get them out. And she would kill Fang.

The least of the Blacks was still a Black.

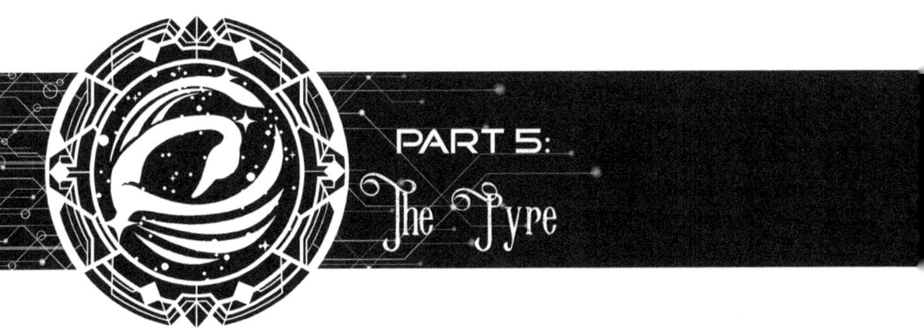

But when the wicked queen stole away the newly born child, and accused the girl, who did not defend herself with a single word, the king had no choice but to bring her to justice, and she was sentenced to die by fire.

When the day came for the sentence to be carried out, it was also the last day of the six years during which she had not been permitted to speak or to laugh, and she had thus delivered her dear brothers from the magic curse. The six shirts were finished. Only the left sleeve of the last one was missing. When she was led to the stake, she laid the shirts on her arm. Standing there, as the fire was about to be lighted, she looked around, and six swans came flying through the air. Seeing that their redemption was near, her heart leapt with joy.

Jacob and Wilhelm Grimm, The Six Swans

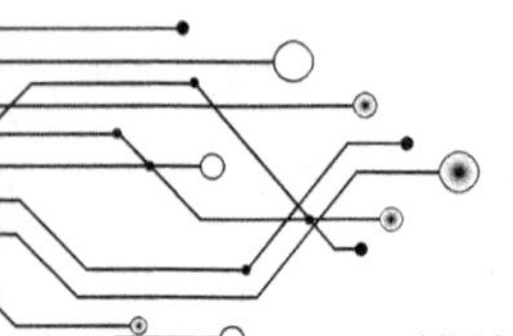

Chapter 25

NIALL AND THE SHARD AGAINST THE RAIDERS

Langston stared at the *Shard's* engine. "This is such a nice ship."

"Thanks," yelled Tara, running by.

"Dad," said Niall, reaching through a mass of cables, trying to get the wrench around the plasma outtake. "Maybe now is not the time." There was an explosion and the ship shook, tossing Niall against the engine block and finally allowing him to close the wrench.

Niall corrected the timing on the outtake valve and the *Shard* lurched forward. The reunion on the *Black Tree* had been short-lived. Langston had quickly determined that the more ships chasing the ion trail, the quicker they could home in on the right path. Unfortunately, Langston had insisted on going along with Niall and Tara. He also kept popping up periodically to run diagnostics on Niall's arm. Niall hadn't had this much trouble getting time alone with a girl since he'd been a teenager. And unfortunately, their last mission had turned up empty. Unless you counted three raider ships full of pirates.

"Niall!" yelled Tara. "I need you up here on the long gun!"

"But," said Langston, as if they weren't being shot at, "it might be better if..."

"Not now, Dad!" barked Niall, brushing past his father on the way up to the gun turret. He swung up the ladder, marveling at the way his new silver hand reacted.

"You've got six," yelled Tara as another explosion shook the hull. She was heaving a barrel-sized shell into the launch chamber of the long gun. He grabbed it with the silver hand, pulling it out of her grasp and loading it easily. "That's six," she repeated, grasping his shoulder. "Get us to the jump point. We'll lose most of them on the jump. We can reload then."

She was sprinting toward the cockpit before he could respond that it wouldn't matter how many raiders stuck with them through the jump. The *Black Tree* was waiting for them on the other side. Tara clearly wasn't used to having backup.

Niall finished the climb into the gun turret and locked himself into the seat. The Be'attle Raiders were swarming them with tiny drone ships, their main ships hanging back, well out of reach of the short-range blasters. Niall set the computer to fire the blasters on a scatter pattern and began siting the long gun. Tara jerked the ship in a downward decent throwing off the drones, then spiraled and began to climb.

"A little warning would be nice on those maneuvers," said Niall over the coms.

"We're running thin on the underbelly shielding. I'm going to turn at 0.6 and three." Tara's voice was tense and clipped, the stress bringing out the Ránfuglar accent.

"Can you hold until the four?" asked Niall.

"Yes, but no further."

"That's all I need," said Niall.

"Gotcha. Turn coming in four, three, two..."

Niall fired. The long gun discharged with a massive explosion that rocked the gun turret. The *Shard* swerved and Niall saw two drones collide with each other in the location where his gun turret had just been.

Over the com, he heard Tara laughing. "Direct hit, *sæta*! she yelled. Keep 'em coming!"

Hopefully, *sæta* wasn't wildly inappropriate. She used it sometimes in bed too. He was going to have to ask her what it meant later. The ship shook again. If they made it to later.

"Hey, kids," said Langston, coming on. "I really think I can make us go faster."

"Not now, Dad," said Niall, as he plotted another targeting solution.

"Another turn coming up!" yelled Tara. "On my mark."

"I need ten more seconds," he yelled back.

"You've got—"

There was an explosion and the entire ship moved sideways.

"Shields weakened below recommended levels," said the computer.

"Maneuvers beginning now," said Tara.

"No! I'm firing!" The ship dove as the long gun fired.

"Sorry!" Tara yelled. "Didn't want to die!"

Niall cursed under his breath.

"Can you target that big cruiser?" she yelled.

"What do you think I'm trying to do?" he yelled back.

He fired again and this time he saw the shell impact against their shields with a purple flare that indicated the shield was close to failure.

"Three minutes to the jump gate! Hit them again and we might make it."

"Don't get too excited! The light ship is swinging around," he yelled back.

"I see it! I see it!" She ran a barrage of blaster fire at the wall of drones as Niall fired again. The light ship countered with a drone cloud that triggered the shell before it reached the ship. He cursed again. He was down to two shells and the gate wasn't getting any closer as Tara was forced into evasive maneuvers.

"Kids, how about now? Because I could really make us go faster."

Niall fired again. It went wide. Over the com, he could hear Tara cursing a blue streak.

"Yeah, Dad. Now."

"Oh, great. Give me just a sec." Langston, as usual, sounded as if he was puttering around in his lab. The stress of impending death never seemed to make a dent in these situations.

"Niall? What did you just tell your dad to—"

Tara cut off as the *Shard* leapt forward. Niall watched as one of the cruiser's long gun shells missed them by inches. "Cruisers coming up behind us!" she yelled.

"Working on it! Give me thirty seconds then burn for the gate." Niall changed the pattern on the blasters and concentrated on targeting the cruiser. The cruiser was gaining on them. He fired the blasters again.

"Any time now!" yelled Tara.

"Just a little closer," he muttered. "Burn now, now, now!" he yelled as the long gun fired.

Tara pushed the ship, and Niall watched as they passed the jump gate outer beacon.

"Starting jump sequence," said Tara.

The beacons flared red, indicating it was no longer safe for anyone to enter the jump zone. Not that a little red light would stop the raiders.

Niall looked back at the cruiser just as the shell impacted. The shield collapsed as he watched. One more hit and the ship would be done for. But, as he watched, the cruiser opened its hanger bay and released the manned stinger ships.

"Faster would be better, angel," he said.

"You want me to screw up the worm hole calcs then keep talking," she snapped.

"Already did them," said Langston. "Here you go."

There was the abrupt taste of orange as the ship began the reality shift. Behind them, Niall watched as the cruiser crossed the beacon line. The jump arc lit up and there was a jagged searing flash of light that left spots in his vision.

"Pull up! Pull up! Pull up!" yelled Matty, as they crossed into the next jump point.

The *Shard* jerked upward and Niall hit the coms. "We've got a cruiser on our tail, Matty, but their shields are down."

"We're on it!"

Niall watched as three of the stinger ships from the *Black Tree* launched Pinwheel rockets. The arc lit up again as the cruiser began to sail through. Its crew saw the rockets heading their way too late. The pinwheels exploded, sending burrowing shrapnel into the hull of the raider's ship. Unable to retreat back into the arc without cracking the ship in half, the raiders were forced forward, into the onslaught.

"Scanners say their systems are already shutting down," said Tara.

"Raider ship, if you wish to surrender, you may. You will be thrown in the brig and dropped at the nearest populated planet. You may also purchase our assistance at very competitive rates." His mother never sounded smug when she made these offers. It was a skill he admired. Perhaps it was because she was telepathic and could tell how much trouble the raiders were actually in.

The raider response was terse, rude and delivered via text. Their communications array was obviously damaged.

"We are posting an arrest beacon. If you are lucky, you may be able to repair yourselves before the authorities arrive. Happy sailing."

Tara burst out laughing. "Your mother kills me."

"Among other people," said Niall, climbing down the ladder.

"Meanwhile," she said, meeting him at the cockpit level and planting a kiss on him, "what did your father do to my ship?"

"What does Dad ever do when left alone with an engine? He made it go faster."

He put his arms around Tara's waist and pulled her to him.

"Hm," said Tara. She didn't look impressed so he kissed her, which made her at least forget about the engine. "What's an angel?" she asked coming up for air. "You called me *angel.*"

"It's a beautiful woman with wings who takes people to the Gods."

"Like a Valkyrie!" The idea seemed to please her.

"I don't know *Valkyrie,*" he replied, kissing along her neck. "I like angel."

"Well, I've sent a few people to the Gods," she agreed. "So, yes, that could be me." She looked pleased with the nickname and he took advantage of the moment to kiss her again.

"Welcome back, Niall," said Matt, over the coms. "You're cleared for landing in Hanger Two."

"Busy," said Niall and Tara giggled.

"Get un-busy," said Mat. "Anwell got back right before you. He's got an eye-witness from the Tetrahino trade base. Best guess is that we're two weeks behind them."

Niall pulled up short. "Two weeks?"

"Yeah, so get your ass on board."

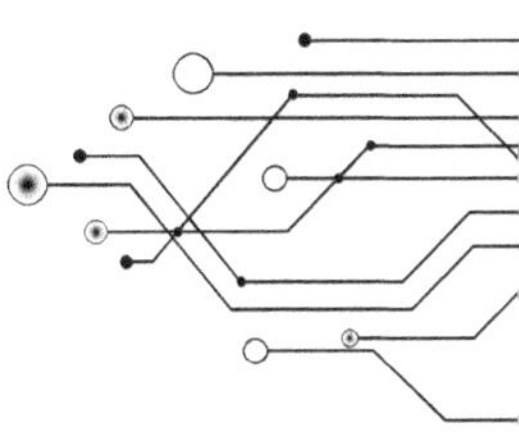

 Chapter 26

JERICHO IN THE DARK

Jericho looked toward what was possibly up and tried to decide if he wanted Fang to visit him today. When she came into the tiny cramped cell, she would bring light. Of course, then she would torture him, but at least there was light. Sometimes a droid came with food and to remove the waste bucket. He assumed that was once a day, but he really didn't know. Judging by the number of times he'd eaten, he thought he had been here sixteen days.

He had no idea if the others were still alive. He thought at least one of them might be, because sometimes he felt a rumbling beneath him in the mine. The mine droids could function without people, but they could not think without people. Mine droids left unattended would cause cave-in after cave-in.

Kodor came to hit him sometimes. But these days, Kodor had the stink of fear on him. He wasn't sure what the reptile thing was scared of, but once when the mine had rumbled particularly loud he'd seen Kodor freeze. Jericho thought that perhaps it was the thing under their feet that scared Kodor. Jericho didn't care about the artifact anymore. He wasn't sure he cared about anything anymore except whether or not there would be light today.

The food arrived. The droid left. Jericho used his belt buckle to scratch another notch in the wall. His hands could barely feel the grooves he left in the wall. His fight with Fang had finally killed most of the nerves. In some ways, that was nice. It took a lot more to make him feel pain.

There was a rumbling in the hallway and he could hear another droid. That was… unusual. The droid paused outside the door. Even more unusual.

The door opened and Jericho raised his hand against the blinding light emanating from the droids main console.

"Do not attempt to escape!" That was the guard robot outside the door. It said that every time the door opened. It also displayed a tangle net and gas weapon that had left him in stinging agony the time he'd tried to push past it. Fang had laughed at him and perhaps that was worse.

The new droid rolled into his cell and the door closed behind it. No Fang or Kodor. Just the droid.

"Base-wide medical check on all humanoids," said the droid cheerfully. "Please extend your right arm."

Jericho didn't move. This had to be some kind of joke. The droid beeped angrily.

"Medical check is required. Please extend your right arm."

Slowly, Jericho did as he was asked. A cuff wrapped around his wrist and the droid began to scan him.

"Health is not optimal. Please take required medicine from the compartment below."

A path of lights traveled from the head of the unit toward the middle where a compartment slid open. Jericho stared at the contents.

"Please take required medicine," said the droid.

With his free hand, Jericho slowly reached out and took the flashlight, screwdriver and protein bar out of the compartment.

"Remember to take medicine on schedule," said the droid.

"I don't have a watch," whispered Jericho, his voice ragged. "How will I know when it's time to… take the medicine."

There was a hiss and a pressure on his wrist.

"Please watch the time sensitive emitter. When it is time to utilize the medicine, the emitter will flash. Do not be alarmed! The emitter is biodegradable and will breakdown after use!"

The cuff retracted and Jericho looked at his wrist. There was now a small, steadily glowing blue dot.

"Thank you for your cooperation!" said the droid. The door rolled open and the droid retreated.

Jericho flicked on the flashlight. Taped to the protein bar was a note that said. FOR NOW. The screwdriver had a note too: FOR THE DOOR. There was a note on the flashlight, but he had to peel it off to read it.

BE READY.

Jericho turned the flashlight on the door. There was an access panel about halfway up. He tore open the protein bar and ate it. He had work to do. Someone was waiting for him.

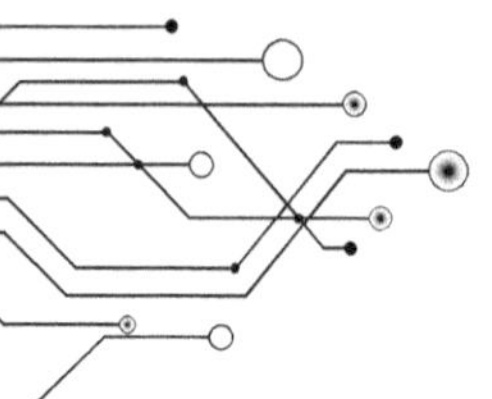

Chapter 27

KEELIA ALONE

It had taken her too long to find Jericho. It was taking her too long to do anything. The only thing that was proceeding with any speed was assembly of the box. And that was good. She should hurry to complete it. The box was important. She should hurry. She needed to...

Keelia stopped and stared at her equation board. She knew now what Fang had meant by dizzying. If she didn't stare directly at the board, the equation would twist, animate, and float out into the room. It was a constant movement in her peripheral vision. When the equation moved was also when she found outside thoughts creeping in. The outside thoughts were a problem. She tried to keep them in check, but it was difficult.

Fang came in. She no longer swept into the room. She came in like she was facing a head wind. Her hair color had only half washed out, the turquoise coming through in streaks, the dress making unhappy ripples. The magnetic forces within the room were now quite strong. Crystal was almost inoperable. Keelia had to take most of her work into rooms further out in the lab, but still, every day, she found herself returning here.

"The others say they will be at the center in six days," Fang said. "When will the box be ready?"

Keelia stared at her.

"Speak," said Fang tiredly.

"Six days," said Keelia, her voice devoid of emotion.

Fang nodded.

"When did you stop living?" asked Keelia. The question had been foremost on her mind now that she had cracked the base code of the dress bug hidden in the supply closet.

"The day I killed Marid," said Fang. "Marid wanted to shut the base down and leave. After Marid died, I replaced my heart. *He* said I had to."

They stared at each other. They had crossed some sort of strange boundary of prisoner and jailer into an equality that they had never been able to previously acknowledge—they were both prisoners.

"Do you think he will let you exist after we set him free?" asked Keelia. She also no longer had to question who *he* was. *He* was the thing waiting for them at the center of the asteroid.

"Why not?" replied Fang with a shrug. "Everyone needs a pet to torture. Although, I'm pretty sure that he'll kill all of you. He doesn't really care much for biologicals."

Keelia nodded. That made sense.

"You could let us go," Keelia suggested, because why not try?

"No," said Fang. "Jericho got everyone out who could get out. The rest of us have to stay until the end."

Keelia nodded again. That was how it felt. She was trying to change that, but that was how it felt.

"Well," said Fang, clapping her hands once, the sound oddly flat and dull. "Six days. Then, at least this will be over." She smiled brightly, patted Keelia's cheek and left the room. Keelia went into the outermost lab where the computer would still work. She had several plans in place, but she'd promised herself she'd wait until the last minute to enact them. They were noticeable actions and any infraction might result in one of the others being punished. But she didn't think she could wait any longer. If she waited, she might not remember that she needed to.

She hit *activate* on all of her pending droid programs and went back to keep an eye on the board. She had to stare at it to keep it from escaping. She just wished she could solve the equation while she was at it. It was starting to really bother her that she hadn't solved it yet.

Somewhere above her in the hangar deck, a droid was loading himself into a launch tube. Hopefully, Kodor wouldn't notice it was missing. Hopefully, someday, her family would find it.

Chapter 28

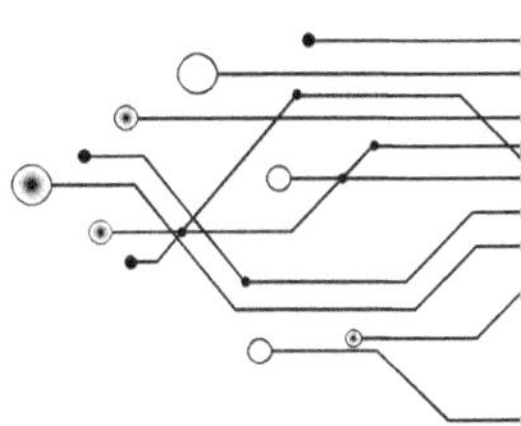

NIALL AND THE BLACK FAMILY

Niall worked the clamp arm and latched it around the droid. It was the same make as the ones they had seen on the moon base, but it was broadcasting a Swan distress code. Gingerly, Niall closed the clamp around the robot and fired thrusters heading back to the *Black Tree*.

He was climbing out of the ship when he looked up and found most of the brothers had assembled. Jed was on shift in the med-bay and Mom was on the bridge. But the others seemed to have come immediately. Anwell looked like he'd just come from the shower and was still pulling his shirt on. Dad barely waited until the engines were cool before reaching for the robot.

Six months. She'd been gone nearly six months. The ion trail had led them this far. The border guards had confirmed that the asteroid had come through, but they had confirmed only three humanoids aboard—two males and one female. The tally didn't make sense. The brothers had seen at least two men and one woman, plus Fang when they'd arrived on the asteroid. Not to mention the alligator thing. There should have been more than three. The number had set off a flood of nerves that Keelia was dead. This was the first real proof that Keelia was still alive.

"Data record," said Langston, extracting a file from the robot.

"Flight deck office," said Matty.

The flight deck officer, a cousin-in-law named Flake, looked shocked to see the six of them in his doorway.

"Need your computer," said Langston.

Flake rolled his chair away from the console. Langston pushed the data record in and pushed play. The next thirty seconds was a soul numbing compilation of Fang Nazari torturing people, including Keelia and Jericho Nazari.

"I don't understand," said Easton. "Why don't they fight back?"

"Wait!" Niall stepped forward, and fumbled at the controls trying to go back on the video. "Where's Tara? Someone get Tara."

"I'm here," said Tara. He rolled the images back until he found what he was looking for. Tara was standing in the doorway and the brothers parted so she could see the image of the Octoparian. She gasped and took an involuntary step forward. "Bruges!"

"I guess that answers the question about whether or not Jericho Nazari is helping her," said Anwell.

"Really?" asked Niall. "You're going with *I told you so* now?"

"I might not have a later," said Anwell, with a shrug. "Got to get them in while I can."

"If you want to keep telling me good news, you go right ahead," said Tara, stepping up to the console to stare at the image. "There's no telling how old the image is though."

"But that's definitely the base," said Niall. "He made it off the ship."

"Doesn't explain why they don't fight back though," said Graves. "Even a pacifist Octoparian wouldn't put up with what she's doing."

"Let it play," said Langston. "Maybe there's something more."

Niall let the video play and tried not to look away when the images of Keelia came up. He didn't have to watch for too much longer. A diagram appeared on the screen along with some text.

NANITE TECHNOLOGY INJECTED SUBCUTANEOUSLY FORCES SUBJECTS TO CARRY OUT COMMANDS FROM THE HOME DATABASE, PERSONIFIED BY FANG NAZARI, THE QUEEN SUBJECT.

Langston grunted in understanding. "Nanites," he said. "They aren't fighting back because they can't. We'll need to get Jed and Declan started on some sort of extraction plan."

The playback flickered and then an image of Keelia appeared. She was staring off screen, then she blinked and stared into the camera. She was dressed in a medical gown, her hair was half-falling out of a braid, and she had claw marks on her arm and face.

"Right, I pushed record. I have to make this now before Fang remembers that she didn't turn me off." Keelia laughed. "And of course, before I forget that I want to make it."

She paused, seeming to stare off into space again.

"Um, I really have tried everything, but I don't think I can actually get out of this. I think I can get the others out. I'm not sure Jericho will leave if I'm not there, but hopefully the others will make him. Mom, if you get this, can you go get them? This is the ship I'm putting them in."

The image switched to a Chimeran ship in the moon base docking bay then back to Keelia.

"The problem is that I haven't finished the equation. I really wish I could get it done, but I'm not thinking very clearly right now. He doesn't want me to." She seemed to focus on the camera again. "If you get this, Dad, I need you to not get interested. I need you to let Mom blow it up. I'm going to let it out. I don't think I can stop it. But it can't get off the asteroid. It's really, really important that it doesn't get out into a populated area. Jericho called it the Soul Sucker and I think that's right."

They all heard Langston's sharp intake of breath that was both recognition and fear.

"I think it would kill everyone. It wants the box because that's the control mechanism. Which, if I could figure out how to work, it might help. Except that I can't. I think maybe it's broken. And the Soul Sucker wants it. If it has that then it can set itself free. And I just keep helping it." Keelia laughed, but as she laughed a tear trickled down her face. "If I stop, then they hurt the others. I tried to do what the other engineers did, but the nanites won't let me. So either I get this right, or a lot of people are going to die. No pressure." She laughed again.

"Anyway, um, if I don't get the explosion right, if you could do me a favor and just come along and kill it, that would be great. And if you can't, then run and don't stop." She stared at the screen again and then nodded. "I think that's it."

The image cut off.

"I've been plotting the droid's trajectory since Niall went out to get it," said Flake, nervously clearing his throat. "Long range scanners pin it to a large asteroid about two days away under standard power. At the speeds we were tracking the droid, I estimate she launched it five days ago."

"If we burn hot, we can be there in half the time," said Mat.

"Yes, but," said Flake, looking even more nervous, "I've been talking to the bridge. The scanners are picking up something else—massive gravitational distortion. It's like there's a dark planet forming out there." Flake hit the display and showed the field distortion.

"Sounds right," said Langston.

"Sounds right?" repeated Matty. "In what way does *that* sound right?" He gestured to the numbers on the screen.

"If Keelia is right, that they're sitting on the Soul Sucker, then yes, those numbers are to be expected. The research I've seen would indicate that it's capable of much more. And, if the containment unit is breaking down, then that is the kind of leakage I would expect."

"Containment unit? I don't understand. What is it?" asked Niall, frowning at Flake's display. He never understood half of what his father said. What he had a clear grasp on was that the gravitational distortion was going to be a problem.

"Legend claims that it's a massive amount of what they used to call dark matter, compressed into a Tesseract Box."

"That's reductive," said Easton. "A tesseract is a box."

"No, a tesseract is the four-dimensional analog of a cube. A Tesseract Box is, in theory, a cube structure that contains a constantly shifting polytope."

"Assuming I understood any of those words," said Niall. "What would that do?"

"It would be a prison," said Langston. "Trapping energy that would be unable to work its way out of the tesseract without someone on the outside creating a porthole or an escape hatch. Legend, myth, research, whatever you want to call it, says that there was a control box that could create such a porthole and through which the energy could be channeled."

"Channeled into what?" asked Anwell.

"Let me guess," said Graves. "Death and destruction."

"Yes, mostly," agreed Langston. "There is a story of someone who used it to repower a sun and save their planet, but mostly, yes, death."

"And Keelia is sitting on top of it," said Easton.

"There's no way the fighter shields can withstand that," said Mat, still looking at Flake's display.

"Mine can," said Tara. "It's got additional shielding and the hull design is intended to be reflective of gravitron bomb waves. It should get us there and back."

They all turned to look at the Ránfuglar's gleaming white ship.

"That's a big risk to take for people who are neither clan nor family," said Langston. The brothers stared at Langston. He was rarely harsh and never politically calculating. They had never heard him say anything like that before.

"Clan and family doesn't…" she hesitated. "Those words don't mean for me what they do for you. I don't have what you have. All I have is my word and my friends. And if Bruges is over there, I'm going to get him out."

Langston eyed her carefully, as if she were a new part he was about to add to one of his inventions. "Exegetics," he said. They all stared at him. "Interpretation is everything," he said as if that helped.

"All right," said Niall, assuming that his father's answer was an affirmative. "Tara's in. Now, how do we kill this Soul Sucker thing?"

"I'm not sure kill is the right word," said Langston.

"Really?" asked Easton. "Because Keelia… I don't know what it's doing to Keelia, but it's doing something. Whatever the Soul Sucker is, I'm pretty sure that killing it is the word I'd use."

Langston looked uncharacteristically grim. "If your description of the asteroid is accurate—that it's riddled with dwarf star alloy, then a sufficient charge should ignite the alloy. That would, I think, disperse the dark matter at enough velocity that it would be essentially dead. I might be able to add a chemical agent as well, which could convert some of the energy to an inert state. Essentially sequester it in asteroids. I wish Keelia was here. She was always good at bonding properties."

Niall could see that his father was already starting to deviate to the tantalizing new invention in his head.

"Can you do it in a day?" asked Niall, trying to sound as much like their mother as he could. Rayna was the only one who could get Langston to focus.

"Oh. Hm. Yes? I think. Well," he said, looking at the display. "I'm going to have to, aren't I? Keelia's rather counting on me." For a moment, Langston's face held a serious expression that exposed his worry for Keelia, then softened to his far-off look that told them he was running equations in his head. "I'm going to the lab," he said. Tara made way for him at the door as he wandered out.

"Flake," said Niall, taking the data record out of the computer, "send the coordinates up to the bridge. I'll go update Mom.

Matty, Tara, can you get together on your ship? I want Matty—er, Mat, up to speed in case we need another pilot." Tara nodded. He looked apologetically at his brother. "I keep trying," said Niall. "But it's a hard habit to break."

"Matty is fine," said Mat, with a smile. "Don't worry about it. Tara, let me go change into my flight suit and I'll meet you down on the flight deck."

"I'll update Jed and then I'll go loiter in Dad's lab," said Graves. "I can usually predict who he'll need to help him with whatever he's inventing. Maybe I can help him go faster."

"I'm going to go to a forward position," said Easton. "Can you send me a rendering of Keelia from that vid? Maybe I can contact her?"

Niall nodded.

"That just leaves me," said Anwell, as his brothers left. "I always feel so useless in these situations."

"Not useless," said Niall. "You're going to pull apart that droid that I brought in and tell us how to kill them. Those droids beat us last time and I will not have that again. I need to you to figure out the weak spots."

Anwell grinned. "On it," he said, already halfway out the door.

Niall looked at Flake and Tara, the only ones left in the room. "Sorry you signed on with the Blacks yet?"

"Not for a minute," said Flake. "I like being on the winning team."

Tara chuckled. "What he said."

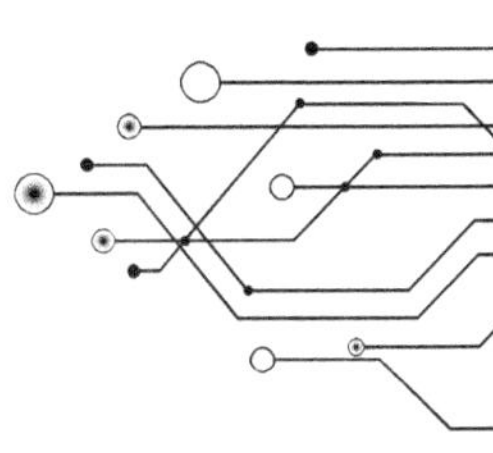

Chapter 29

JERICHO ESCAPES

Jericho woke up to a flashing light. He raised his hand to block it and realized that the light was coming from his hand. The tiny blue dot the medical droid had injected into him was now flashing rapidly.

He lunged for the flashlight and screwdriver and scrambled to the access panel. He'd done most of the work already. He adjusted the screwdriver, ripped off the panel face and found the two contact points he was looking for. The door lurched sluggishly open as he connected them. Outside, the hall was dark, and no sound came from the droids beyond the door. He cautiously stepped out. The droids' central display panel scrolled in a continuous message: MAINTENANCE MODE.

The hallway was dark because neither Fang nor the droids appeared to require light. He flicked on his flashlight and the beam swept across the far wall of the passageway. He was about to pull the light away when he realized that there was something written on the far wall. He put the flashlight back and saw an arrow pointing left.

He followed the instructions, inching around the droids. There was another arrow at the next junction and then another. He came out into a service area, with overhead lights that were just beginning to flicker back to life, and found a med-droid waiting for him.

"Caution! Caution!" said the droid. "You are entering a

contaminated area! You must receive an inoculation before proceeding!"

Jericho extended his arm and the robot extended its own with a hypo-spray at the end, quickly injecting him. He felt almost nothing, and then his arms twitched as if the nanites under his skin were not happy with whatever had just been added to his bloodstream.

"Thank you for your cooperation!" exclaimed the robot. "Please proceed to the hangar bay."

The hangar bay was on the list of forbidden areas. Previously, even thinking about the hangar bay would cause the nanites to dig into him a little bit.

"I'm going to go to the hangar bay," Jericho said out loud. Nothing moved under his skin.

"That is excellent, sir!" said the med-droid.

"Actually, I'm going to the weapons locker first," said Jericho.

"We recommend the hangar bay, sir," said the droid. "But please proceed."

Jericho ignored the droid and began to run toward the weapons locker. The lights continued to flicker as he ran and the deck plating under his feet was shaking. He slammed through the door into the testing area and straight into Bruges's tentacle.

Jericho slammed to the floor and looked up at the Octoparian.

"Sorry Jericho," whispered Bruges, picking him up. "I thought you were Kodor."

Bruges set him on his feet and Jericho looked around. Pavel emerged from the weapons locker carrying a gun and Jericho's glaive.

"Jericho?" he asked, sounding uncertain.

"That bad, huh?" asked Jericho, trying for a smile. He realized that between the ragged beard, blood and grime, he was probably unrecognizable.

Pavel didn't respond, but instead tossed him the glaive. Jericho nearly missed catching it because he couldn't feel it hit his hand.

"Where's Phaedra?" Jericho asked.

"Here," she said, stepping out of the locker, tucking a stick-like weapon into her belt. He recognized it as the weapon she'd been captured with.

"Where's Keelia?" he asked looking around the room.

"She's meeting us at the hangar bay," said Pavel. "The droid said to go directly there, but we thought stopping here first might be better."

"Me too," agreed Jericho. "Where's Fang?"

Phaedra and Pavel exchanged looks. "We've reached the center," said Phaedra. "It's a cube. A giant cube. About twenty feet tall with equations and writing all over it. Nothing we have will scan it. The computers just keep saying nothing is there. But we can all feel the heat coming out of it—so there's something inside. We said we needed a special set of charges to blow the wall, and Keelia got the droids to load the charges with dwarf star alloy."

"That will blow the whole damn asteroid," said Jericho, gaping.

"That's what we hope," said Pavel. "Fang wants to blow the

wall herself. This is our window of opportunity. We hit the hangar bay, take Thanh Vien's ship and we fly like hell."

Jericho nodded. "Will we be able to go to the hangar bay?"

"We all got to the weapons locker," said Phaedra, with a shrug. "Whatever Keelia came up with, it seems to be working."

Jericho nodded again. "Good. Then let's get Keelia and get the hell out of here."

The trip up to the hangar bay was bizarrely quiet. The droids they met along the way were all in Maintenance Mode. As they approached down the main promenade on level one, Jericho felt his steps quickening at the same time that his heart began to sink. He didn't see Keelia anywhere. Everything appeared just as it had when they'd gathered to meet Thanh.

"Where is she?" whispered Pavel nervously.

"Maybe she's waiting for us in the hanger bay?" suggested Phaedra, looking equally worried.

Abruptly, the lights went out and then came back on and they all heard the whir of droids coming back to life.

"Run," said Jericho. They sprinted toward the bay doors only to see Kodor had beat them there. He had an army of robots behind him.

"You fail!" he laughed. "So close, but I will take the ship and you will all die!"

"Where is Keelia?" demanded Jericho.

"You want girl, you go find her," said Kodor, slapping his tail on the ground. "I take ship. You all die." Behind Kodor, the fifty or so one-wheeled droids rolled slightly on their spheres, shifting back and forth as if nervous.

"You are not taking that ship," said Phaedra, flicking out her weapon. The stick telescoped outward and a long, curved blade snicked out from the top.

"Stop me," said Kodor, and he tapped a command on his com bracelet, and the wide doors began to open ponderously. Then he flicked a claw at the droids, gesturing them toward the prisoners.

Bruges roared in rage, ran forward and seized the nearest robot. Flinging it overhead, the droid bulls-eyed into the access panel by the doors. There was a screech as the doors ground to a halt. Kodor snarled angrily and came back to fight.

Jericho squeezed his hand and the glaive came to life with the beautiful singing note that he loved. He cut through the nearest droid and then another, but as he lifted his blade for another strike, there was an enormous silence that hit everything. He watched Pavel try to yell and no sound came out. Then the gravity flipped and he crashed into the wall.

He'd felt this before, when a ship he was on was struck by a graviton war head. He rolled to avoid taking a droid to the head and ran along the wall toward Kodor. There was another silence and the gravity flipped again. He jumped, preparing for the shift, and landed on his feet as the gravity went back to the floor. He was nearly to Kodor. Bruges was flinging droids angrily as he clung to an anchored light fixture. Phaedra and Pavel were clinging to a wide potted palm. Kodor saw Jericho coming and ran for the door again.

Then the doors exploded.

Jericho hit the floor as a shard of metal rocketed by his head.

He raised his head and blinked through smoke. People were standing in the doorway. They wore black space suits with gold swans on the chest. Behind them, an angel was hovering in gleaming white with silver wings. Bruges let out a bizarre yodel of happiness and began running along the wall toward the newcomers. Jericho didn't have time to think about any of that—Kodor was getting away.

He reached out and grabbed Kodor by the tail. Kodor's massive tail flicked, flipping Jericho with a hard and unexpected jerk. Jericho rolled, scrambling as he felt Kodor's hard claws grab him by the ankle. Jericho looked back and kicked at Kodor's stubby fingers and then upward into the uneven row of teeth in his long maw. Kodor let go and opened his jaw, hissing in pain and anger. Jericho kicked again, this time in the throat. He pulled himself to his feet and punched, feeling the repressed rage and anger in every hit as it made contact. Kodor staggered back, his tail swinging out, but this time Jericho jumped and avoided it. Closing in again, he kicked out, but Kodor swung his heavy head, cracking his skull against Jericho's with a blinding impact. Shaking his head, Jericho raised his glaive, knowing he only had seconds before Kodor struck again. He braced for impact, but instead heard an angry scream from Phaedra and then Kodor bellowed in pain. He looked down and saw that Phaedra had cut off Kodor's tail. Jericho reached out and grabbed Kodor by the throat. "Where is she?" he yelled, holding the glaive inches from Kodor's snout. Jericho had imagined this moment a hundred times, but he found he no longer cared about Kodor.

Kodor's eyes showed white around the edges. "The mines," he hissed, his red tongue flicking out. Jericho dropped him.

He looked at Phaedra.

"You won't reach her in time," Phaedra said.

"Get off the base," he told her.

Jericho turned around and realized that at least some of the people were Keelia's crew. Her family, she'd called them. "Wait," said their Captain, but Jericho didn't have time to wait.

There was the rolling silence that indicated another gravity shift and Jericho leaped. The gravity flipped to the ceiling and Jericho landed, already running.

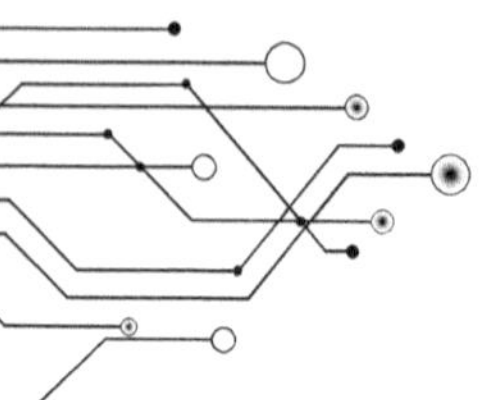

Chapter 30

KEELIA FACES THE FIRE

Keelia stared at the box as she walked. She was so close to finishing the damn equation. If Fang would just let her stop and concentrate, she was certain she could do it. But every time Keelia paused, Fang would grab her arm and pull her forward.

Keelia?

Keelia stopped and looked around for Easton.

"Keep moving," snarled Fang.

Keelia, wait for us.

She looked around again and then down at the box she held. She twisted it in her hands, looking at the faces, trying to trace the path of the equation.

"I really need to finish this," said Keelia.

"You already finished it," said Fang impatiently. "We need to go give it to him."

"Right," said Keelia. "Of course."

She hesitated again. Easton had wanted her to wait and she couldn't help feeling that she'd forgotten something important. Fang slapped her on the back of her head, pushing her face closer to the box. Keelia started walking again. Obviously, nothing was more important than the box.

Keelia stumbled and her eyes moved away from the box. For the first time, she realized that she was in the mines.

"When did we come down here?"

Fang looked at her pityingly. "Never mind that. Just keep

walking." Fang's hair was now back to turquoise and her dress seemed to have taken on a new style. It was as if she had dressed up for the occasion. But somehow it only emphasized how lacking in color her skin was and how inhuman she looked.

"If we're in the mine, shouldn't the others be here? Where's Jericho?" Keelia looked around as if expecting him to suddenly appear.

"Jericho's dead, dear," said Fang.

Keelia stared at Fang and then stopped walking. "No," she said.

"Yes," said Fang, reaching back and trying to drag her.

"No," said Keelia.

"Everyone's going to die. We're all dead," said Fang. "Just keep walking."

"No," said Keelia, stubbornly, although her feet shuffled forward an inch on their own. "No, I won't until you tell me where—" Keelia gasped as the box emitted a shockwave of silence. Keelia dropped it and stared at the cube in the dust. She needed to leave. Now. Had she really heard Easton? How far away were they?

"Pick it up," demanded Fang, shaking her by the arm. Above them there was a grinding noise of scraping rock and twisting metal. "Pick it up!" Fang screamed into her face.

"You can't touch it, can you?" asked Keelia. "That's why you couldn't put it together yourself."

Fang's dress thrashed angrily. "Pick it up," hissed Fang, and Keelia felt the burning tingle of the nanites in her throat. Another wave of silence rolled out of the box and Fang twisted, her skin and dress rippling as if caught in some unseen current.

Keelia turned and ran a few steps toward the mine entrance. Fang howled angrily, and Keelia felt the burning pain in her throat. She dropped to her hands and knees, panting.

There was a rustle as Fang pulled herself back together and pursued Keelia up the tunnel.

"You will pick up the box!" Fang stooped over Keelia. The dress wrapped around Keelia's waist, picking her up and carrying her. Then she was dropped back in front of the box.

Keelia stared at the box. She was so close to finishing the damn equation. If Fang would just let her stop and concentrate, she was certain she could do it.

"I really need to finish this," said Keelia.

"You can finish it," said Fang. "You just need to take it the center of the asteroid."

Keelia nodded and stood up, preparing to pick up the cube. The box twitched again and more silence poured out. Fang gnashed her teeth and twisted, her skin stretching and compressing.

"Is it supposed to do that?" asked Keelia. She didn't feel whatever it was that Fang did and that seemed weird.

"No. It's broken. That's why we need to take it to him. Remember?"

"Right," said Keelia. "But maybe I should take it back to the lab and try and fix it?"

"No," snapped Fang, pushing Keelia. "Take it to him."

Keelia stumbled forward. She thought she heard Easton again, but he was dim over the rushing sound in her ears. She turned the box again, trying to find what she was missing. If she could just solve it, she might be able to figure out how to control it. The air was getting warmer and the dirt under her feet no longer felt cold—it felt hot like a beach she had visited once while at school.

Keelia blinked, remembering the blue sky. She slowed down, trying to picture what the water had felt like against her skin.

Keelia. Stop.

Fang's hand closed around her arm and began to pull her. Keelia wanted to resist, but found that she couldn't. The memory of blue sky slipped away and all that remained was the cool, heavy feeling of the cube in her hands. The raised and indented lettering trapped her fingers as she caressed the box.

They rounded a corner and ahead of them was a wall. Keelia stared at it in surprise. It was an exact replica of the box in her hand, but in the wall was a giant crack. A piece had already fallen away and through the crack could be seen a burning yellow that smoked and roiled like plasma.

"Yes," hissed Fang.

Keelia felt a numbness spread out along her limbs.

"Go," said Fang, pushing Keelia. Keelia took one step and stopped again.

"Fang!"

Keelia knew that was Jericho, but she couldn't turn around. She could hear running feet, but she couldn't stop staring at the crack in front of her. The box in her hand gave another twitch and the silence rolled out again. Fang froze, gasping in pain. Ahead of her, another piece of the wall fell away. Through the wall, a dark spot appeared, like an iris in an eye.

The was a crash and Fang hurtled through the air as if thrown.

Jericho came after her. He was carrying the weapon that he'd had the night of their escape attempt. It fit his hand like a glove with a glowing blade coming out of it. He hit Fang in the dress, slicing bits of it off.

Keelia could see by the grimace on Fang's face that she was trying to activate Jericho's nanites, but Jericho gave no indication that he felt anything. That meant that her inoculation had worked. Keelia thought she should probably care about all of that, but she couldn't stop staring at the yellow eye. It wanted the box. She took a step closer.

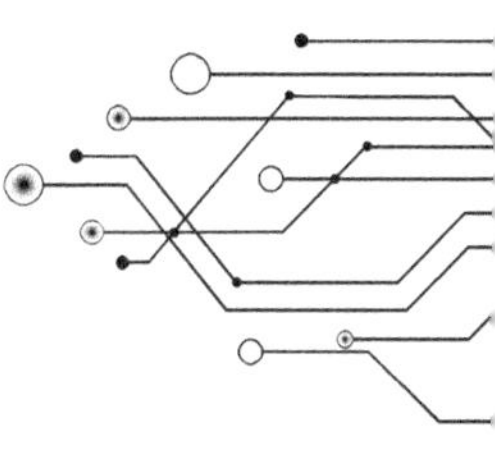

Chapter 31

JERICHO AT THE END

Keelia took a step forward, her eyes fixed on the wall in front of her, and Jericho was forced to stop his swing before it sliced into her. Fang laughed and he saw the dress wrap around Keelia's ankles. He sliced at the dress and the nanites separated and then hurried to get back to their queen, scurrying like ants across the rock. Jericho grabbed at Keelia, her face blank and expressionless as she took another step closer to the wall. She showed no recognition of either him or his hand on her. He grabbed her by the arm and swung her around as Fang reached for her again. There was the sound of running feet behind them and Jericho glanced around in time to see the Captain of Keelia's ship rounding the corner. Jericho shoved Keelia at him as Fang's dress swept over his head.

He could feel the nanites crawling over his face and then there was an impact along one side of his face. He felt a hand grab his shirt and rip him free of the dress. The Captain of the *Black Light* pulled Jericho away from the dress, holding him in the air with ease, firing a blaster at the trailing edge of nanites that sought to hold on to him. Jericho saw another tendril of the dress pick up a rock and hurl it at them. Jericho twisted his glaive and brought up a hammer, swinging it at the rock. The impact shattered the rock and sent both of them flying backward.

Jericho looked around for Keelia. She was on her hands and knees. For a moment their eyes connected, and she looked like herself—scared, but still Keelia. And then she saw the wall. Her eyes glazed over and she stood up and picked up the box she'd been carrying.

The Captain yelled her name, but she didn't hear him. Fang threw him against the wall, then stepped aside to let Keelia pass.

"You're going to lose, Jericho," said Fang laughing. "You can't save her. You can't save any of them."

The Captain stood up and threw a grenade at Fang. Jericho knew the dress would catch it, but it would take a lot of her resources to deal with it. He launched himself at Fang, slicing at her arm as she caught him. The arm dropped away and then began to disintegrate into nanites and reabsorb into the dress. The grenade went off somewhere inside the dress and Fang staggered. Jericho kicked her in the chest and swung the glaive again. For a moment she was cut, and the pieces seem to struggle to rejoin each other. He turned, picked up Keelia and ran back up the mine shaft. The dress caught him by the ankle and he went sprawling, throwing Keelia down again. The Captain was firing again as Jericho sliced at the tendril holding his ankle. Another tendril shot out and latched around the Captain's throat. Jericho watched in surprise as the Captain reached up and crushed the tendril with his hand—nanites falling away like dust.

Keelia was struggling to push herself upright, but her hands and arms jerked spasmodically, as if she wasn't controlling them herself. He looked back at the Captain again. The dress was swarming at him from multiple angles.

Jericho jerked himself to his feet and ran back as the dress lashed at the Captain again. The blond man glanced back at

Keelia, now attempting to stand. "If she reaches the wall, we're all dead!" he yelled, just as the dress shot out, covering his face.

Jericho sliced the tendril away and raised his arm again and again as Fang slashed at them. He didn't care about all of them; he cared about Keelia. The Captain was grabbing everything he could reach and squeezing, crushing nanites in his grasp. It was a nice trick—Jericho wished he knew how to replicate it—but it was slow.

Jericho sliced again. They needed a plan. "Shoot Fang in the head!" he yelled to the Captain. "I'll cover you, but keep firing!" The Captain nodded and did as Jericho said. Fang had dropped all pretense at humanity and her skin had taken on a silvery white hue, the delineation between her and the dress nothing more than a faded line of color. She struck at them again, but the Captain was a sure shot and Fang was forced into retreat, blinded by the blaster fire and forced to repair herself again and again. Jericho pressed their advantage, edging forward. He was dimly aware of a strange sound behind them, but it didn't register as important until he heard the high-pitched whine of artillery coming online.

The Captain of the *Black Light* shoved Jericho, tackling him into a wall. "Light her up, angel!"

There was a blue flash of plasma fire. Jericho glanced back and saw the angel was carrying an enormous gun. He hadn't known angel's carried guns, but then he wasn't very religious. On the other hand, this *did* seem like a damn miracle.

Fang dodged the first shot, but then the angel fired again and Fang staggered, a hole in her body where her heart should have been. She stared down at herself in seeming surprise and Jericho leapt forward, raising his glaive, and sliced through her neck. Her head bounced off her shoulder and he kicked the body, sending it flying into the wall, where it stuck, obscuring the yellow eye. He looked down at the head and saw that she was blinking at him, her face enraged.

The Captain of the *Black Light* scooped up the head and hurled it at the wall. The dress tried to catch it, but the entire body was starting to disintegrate, the nanites dropping away like dust.

"Jericho."

He wheeled around immediately. Keelia was standing next to the angel, but he had eyes only for her. She looked him in the eye and smiled. "Smash it," she said.

His gaze dropped to the box in her hands. He flipped his weapon around, spinning it in his fist and the blade came up as an axe. He raised it over his head and brought it down on the box. For a moment, time stood still, and the box pieces held together. Then it shattered with the force of a bomb.

With the breach of the box, Keelia dropped to the ground as if he'd struck her instead of the box. Behind him, Fang began to scream, yellow light burning through the dress. He could feel the nanites under his skin begin to move. He turned to the Captain of the *Black Light*. He was going to need help for this.

"Charges," Jericho yelled over Fang's keening, pointing at the explosive droids. The man nodded—Jericho took two steps and then staggered. His skin was shredding as the nanites sought escape. Jericho looked up at the burning eye. He wasn't going to make it. He wasn't going to be able to get them out. He looked at Keelia—nanites were pouring out of her mouth, like black blood.

More of the Swans were running into the cavern. The Captain of the *Black Light* was yelling something and pointing. But Jericho couldn't make out the words. The angel was bending over Keelia, then she picked up Keelia and flew away.

He felt a hand grab his shoulder. He raised the glaive, but the Captain knocked it back down.

"Your turn," said the man. Jericho didn't know what that meant. He looked down and hands were picking him up. They pushed him onto a mining skiff.

"Turn the weapon off," someone yelled. He did as they asked, because he couldn't think of a reason not to. So what if he died? Keelia was already gone.

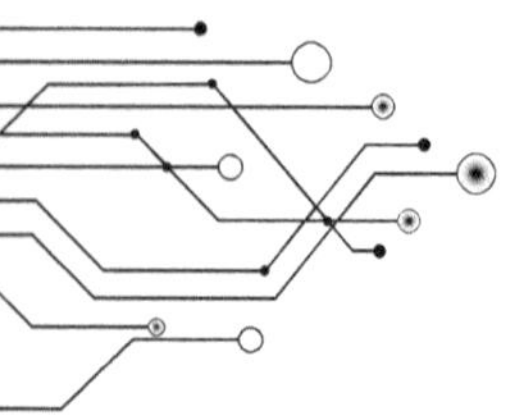

Chapter 32

KEELIA IN THE DARK

Keelia sat on a rock and stared at the equation. She was so close to solving it. If she could just solve for a whole number on the left…

"Keelia," said a nervous voice. She looked up and was surprised to see Easton.

"Easton! There you are! Where have you been?"

"It took me awhile to find you," said Easton. "I've come to take you home."

"Oh good. I want to go home," said Keelia. "But first, I need to solve the equation."

"Equation?" Easton repeated.

"The equation," said Keelia, pointing.

"I don't see an equation," said Easton nervously.

"No? It is really complex, I guess. Can you go get Dad? He would help."

"No, it's time to go home," said Easton, he put out a hand as if to pull on her arm, but didn't actually touch her. "We have to go now."

"Not just yet," said Keelia impatiently.

"Yes, now," said Easton, stepping between her and the equation.

"Easton!" she said, craning to look around him. He seemed to be sweating.

"Keelia, baby?"

"Mom!" Keelia looked around in surprise. "Mom, tell Easton to move."

"No, baby, it's time to come home." Her mother went to stand next to Easton.

"But I'm so close to solving it," said Keelia.

"Solving what?" asked Rayna, glancing over her shoulder at the equation.

"The equation. Honestly, can one of you go get Dad? I know we can figure it out."

"No, Keelia," said her mother firmly. "It's time to go now." She and Easton took a step closer to her. Keelia stood up in annoyance.

"I don't know why you won't let me just finish this."

"You can finish it after we get home," said Rayna.

"I'll have lost all momentum," grumbled Keelia, turning around. Easton and her mother promptly took a step closer to her, herding her up the tunnel. Keelia stopped and looked at the walls in surprise. They were flickering yellow, as if there was a fire behind them. Keelia looked back. There was only the equation, spinning and floating in the infinity symbol. She looked back at the walls, perplexed.

"Keep moving, Keelia," said her mother. "Your brothers are waiting for you."

Keelia took a step and then stopped, struck by a staggering memory of her brothers being lost in space. "No, they died," she gasped. "I killed them in space." She turned around and grabbed for Easton, but couldn't seem to connect.

"No, we're fine," said Easton reassuringly.

"You're fine?" She looked at her mother. "They're fine?"

"Yes," said Rayna. "All of them came home. The memory in your head isn't real. You helped them escape and they came home." Rayna pointed toward the tunnel and Keelia shook her head and walked a few more feet. "It seemed so real," she said.

"But it's not," said Easton. She looked back at him. He was definitely sweating. "I'm right here."

"But…" Keelia frowned. Something wasn't right. "But what happened after you left?"

"Nothing much. We got a little hung up in a Rantarian Slave Mart, and Niall had a little bit of a problem with his arm. But other than that, everything went fine."

That sounded just like her brothers. *A little hung up*, indeed. They probably ended up burning the place to the ground.

"That's good," said Keelia. Easton's understatement was infinitely more reassuring than if he'd attempted to go into detail. She walked forward, Rayna and Easton walking inches behind her. Keelia reached out for the wall for support; her legs felt incredibly heavy.

"Mom," she said, breathing heavily, "did they adjust the atmosphere down here? It's really hot."

"Keep going, Keelia," said Rayna.

She stopped again, struck by a memory of Phaedra being stabbed through the heart. Then Pavel being killed by Kodor. Then Bruges, his arms ripped off. Then Jericho, with Fang's hand in his chest, pulling out his heart.

Keelia dropped to the ground.

"Keelia," said her mother. "You have to get up."

"I can't," sobbed Keelia.

"You have to," said Rayna, who sounded panicked. Rayna never panicked.

"Hey Keels," said a third voice, almost the same as Easton's.

"Graves," she sobbed, reaching for him. He would understand. "Graves, they're dead! He's dead!"

"Who's dead?" he asked, kneeling down next to her. The memories of her friends' deaths filled her head again. "Ah. The good looking guy with the badass axe thing."

"He's dead. They're all dead," she sobbed. Why wouldn't any of them help her?

"No," said Graves. "I just saw them. The Octoparian was flinging robots around like pick-up-sticks. The green-haired chick was slicing and dicing like alligator was on the menu. The belter kid was going to town with a hammer and a blaster. And the cutie with the axe was kicking ass and taking names. Come on," he beckoned. "We can go see them. It's just a little further."

Keelia crawled forward. The heat behind her was growing.

"That's right," said Graves. "Just a little further."

It was getting darker.

"Good job, Keelia," said her mother as the light flickered out.

"Eight," said Keelia. "The number I needed was eight."

As a punishment, the wicked queen was tied to the stake and burned to ashes.

Jacob and Wilhelm Grimm, The Six Swans

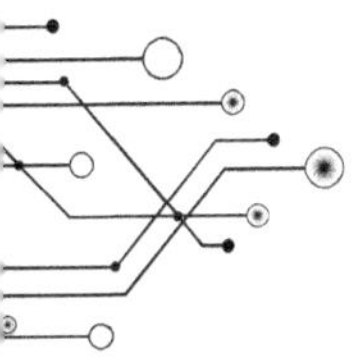

Chapter 33

NIALL AND KEELIA

Niall looked around the construction bay, finally spotting Keelia at the top of the scaffolding, staring out the windows into space. He jumped up and caught the metal bar above his head and began to climb up. He had almost reached the top when Keelia leaned over the edge.

"If you're here for a meaningful chat, you can turn around right now."

"What are you talking about?" he asked, pausing.

"Everyone keeps asking, *how are you* and trying to have meaningful chats," she said.

"Oh," said Niall, swinging up onto the platform beside her. "Yeah, I'm getting those too. Also, hugs."

"Dear Gods below! If Graves hugs me one more time, I swear I will not be responsible for my actions!"

Niall chuckled. "Why do you think I'm hiding up here with you?"

"Even Anwell," said Keelia. "And I rely on him to be an asshole. They're driving me crazy!"

"Yeah, I'm not getting that from Anwell. He just keeps complaining that I can work out in half the time now."

"Well, yeah, but what happens if your regular arm gets too bulky? You'll look all lopsided and have to get a new metal arm. I don't think he's thought about the maintenance aspect."

"Well, neither had I until you just pointed it out," said Niall. "Thanks a bunch."

Keelia giggled. Then her fingers twisted together in a knot. "I do feel guilty about your arm," she said.

"Why?"

"Because I squished your pod." He could tell that she was serious. Behind Graves, she had always been his most tender-hearted sibling.

"Phaedra says it was a mechanical malfunction probably caused by that Soul Sucker thing," said Niall. "All your friends say everything had been disintegrating for months. If it hadn't been for you, we wouldn't have gotten away at all."

"Yeah?" She didn't look convinced. "I still feel guilty."

"Well, stop," he said.

"If you say so," she said, and leaned against his metal arm, her head resting against his shoulder. Despite the hugs, not many of his family were quite willing to touch it yet, let alone with affection. He smiled.

"I saw your girlfriend today," she said, still staring at the stars.

"Yeah?" Niall could tell she was teasing him a little, or she would have just said Tara's name.

"She and Bruges came into the med-bay and played cards with me."

"And?"

"And nothing. That was it. No meaningful chats, no *how are you's*, no special hugs. She just kicked my ass at cards and promised to bring me some booze if Declan and Jed didn't let me out soon. It was nice. I like her. And Bruges likes her. Although, I think she may also be feeling a little over-hugged. It's hard to avoid when the hugger has eight arms."

Niall laughed. "Don't let her fool you. She likes it."

"Is she sticking around?"

"I hope so," said Niall. "We haven't really talked about it. I get the feeling that sticking around isn't something she's done a lot of and it kind of freaks her out."

"Well, just make it easier for her to stick around than to leave," said Keelia and Niall laughed.

"I'll keep that in mind. Meanwhile, if we're talking relationships, I did *not* know that you liked tough guys. I thought you were into those floppy-haired smart boys."

"Jericho is smart!" protested Keelia.

Niall gave her a look. "Keels, I saw him backflip through a gravity shift, land it, cut off a droids head, run through the entire base, battle a crazy bug lady and then try and walk it off when a swarm of nanites exploded out of his chest. Pretty sure he's a tough guy."

"I didn't say he wasn't tough," she said, a smile quirking up one side of her mouth. "I said he was smart."

"Yeah, well, at least he's got the floppy hair. Is he going to stick around?"

She blushed and looked away. "Niall, up until… whenever many days ago that was, I wasn't actually able to speak to him. Like literally, I had to write messages. We covered a lot of ground, but most of it was on how to escape."

"And making out?" suggested Niall.

"Shut up," said Keelia, blushing harder. "My point is that we haven't exactly had time to work out what happens next."

"Well, Phaedra gave us the coordinates for his home planet. We're a few weeks away from having to make any decisions. You've got time to talk, among other things. You know, as soon as he's conscious."

"Seriously, shut up." Her com bracelet beeped, and she checked the message with a groan. "Stupid Jed says I have to come back for another dose of whatever. Why can't they just let me be better?"

"Well, probably because you and the others had nanites popping out of you like popcorn, and the blood loss, tissue and nerve damage all take some time to recover from? And of course, also because you were imprisoned and tortured for six months and then a Soul Sucker almost ate your brain," he said.

"Well, sure, if you put it like that, it sounds bad," said Keelia, starting to climb down.

"Keels," he said, leaning over the scaffolding and looking down at her. "It sounds bad, because it was bad. Do you realize the megaton of explosive power we had to use to disperse the energy of that thing? Not to mention whatever the hell Dad invented to bind some of it to the asteroid chunks."

"I know," said Keelia, looking up. "I saw Dad's equations. But I was unconscious for that part, so it wasn't that big of a deal for me."

Niall opened his mouth to say that the explosives hadn't been the hard part. Then he shook his head. He was pretty sure that his tiny, tender-hearted sister was also a tough guy.

"You know what the worst part is?" she asked when they were on the ground. "When Mom, Easton, and Graves came to get me or my brain or whatever, I actually solved the damn equation. And now I can't remember any of it."

"Pretty sure that's for the best," said Niall.

"Probably," she agreed. "But it's still annoying."

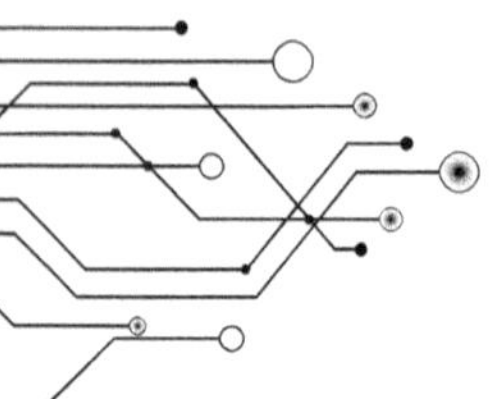

Chapter 34

JERICHO IN THE MED-BAY

Jericho opened his eyes. He was in the med-bay. Where were the others? Where was Keelia? There were tubes in his arms. He could see that, but he couldn't feel it. What was Fang doing to them now?

He sat up. That went well. At least he could move. And if he could move, then he didn't have to stay here. He began pulling the tubes out. He had to find Keelia and the others.

"No, no, no!" yelled a blond man coming around the corner. Jericho pulled faster. He couldn't feel his hands, but they did respond to commands, like making a fist. He hit the blond guy and jumped off the table.

He made it out of the med-bay before things started to go wrong. The floors were shiny. The walls were the wrong color. They were *a* color, for one thing. Everything looked different. What was Fang doing?

His memory sparked with an image of Fang, her face twisted in pain, her body disintegrating.

He stumbled and reached for the wall for support. He heard the sound of laughter and looked up. Keelia was walking toward him with the Captain of the *Black Light*. He had his arm around her shoulders and she leaned into him affectionately. Jericho felt light headed.

Keelia's eyes widened as she saw him and started to run in his direction, struggling to catch him as he fell over.

"Jed!" she yelled at someone behind him as they sank to the floor. "What the hell, Jed? Why did you let him out of the med-bay?"

"I didn't let him do anything," snapped the blond man coming into view. "He woke up, yanked out all his ports, punched me in the face and walked out."

"Well, I think we've all wanted to do that," said the Captain, leaning over Jericho.

"You know what—" began Jed, looking offended.

"Can you two argue later?" demanded Keelia.

"Yes," said the Captain. "Come on Jed, let's get him up."

"Where are the others?" demanded Jericho, refusing to let go of Keelia.

"I think they all went to the pool," said Keelia.

"Wha—?"

"Quick," said Jed, "while he's processing that one."

"The pool?" Jericho repeated.

"Well, Bruges hasn't been properly in water since the tank cracked. And did you know that Phaedra's hair filters UV light through chlorophyll to produce extra oxygen? So she's under a sun lamp. And I think Pavel's just enjoying getting hit on by my cousins."

Jericho tried to focus on Keelia's explanation as he found himself being picked up and half-carried back into the med-bay, but it made no sense. He looked from Jed to the Captain. "Who are you?" he asked.

"That's Jed," said the Captain.

"And that's Niall," said Jed. "We're Keelia's brothers."

"Didn't she mention us?" asked Niall, hefting Jericho back up on to the bed.

"Oh, very funny," said Keelia.

"It was a little funny," said Jericho, blinking at the ceiling. He still felt light headed and the sensation hadn't returned to his hands and arms.

"Don't encourage them," said Keelia, leaning over him. She was smiling at him.

"You sound exactly how I thought you would," Jericho said and Keelia laughed.

"For crying out loud," said Jed in irritation. "That was brand new skin." Jed was poking at his arm, trying to get the medical ports reinstalled. "You're in the middle of a cycle. I can't do a new graft. You're going to have a scar!"

Jericho blinked at him and at his arm. His arm did indeed look less scarred than he remembered. But if his friends were at the pool and Keelia was here, it wasn't like scars mattered in any way.

"Who cares?" he said.

Jed jabbed the port needle into his arm until the muscle reacted. "Ow!" said Jericho

"Apparently, Jed cares," said Keelia, still smiling.

"Yes, well, Jed cares so much that he's going to do this," said Jed, picking up a spray vial and jabbed Jericho in the neck.

"I don't think—" began Jericho, as he felt whatever Jed had given him hit his system, but it was already too late, darkness was closing over him.

When he woke up, Jed was sitting on the bed next to him,

shuffling through various data chips and typing into a tablet. The med-bay was quiet and mostly dark. Jed had the rumpled air of doing paperwork that he hated.

"Where'd everybody go?" asked Jericho as he watched Jed jump in surprise.

"Son of a… How do you keep waking up? You should be out for at least another four hours."

"What are you using?" asked Jericho. "Something with Sonos-X?"

"Yes, it's standard. Why?" Jed pulled the scanner out of the wall and began taking readings.

"Resistance therapies," said Jericho. "Sonos-X can also be used for information extraction. Everyone in the Chimera military gets treated."

Jed grunted unhappily. "Well, unfortunately, with the amount you've got in your system, I can't use anything else to put you back under."

"It's fine," said Jericho. "I feel fine. I just can't feel my arms."

"Yeah," said Jed, popping up another piece of equipment and attaching it to Jericho's left arm. "That's the problem. Your nerve damage was extensive. We had to replace a bunch of the nerves in your arms and chest. The ports were feeding the growth matrix. They have completed the re-growth, but you're due for the reconnection cycle shortly."

"What does that mean?" asked Jericho as his right hand twitched with a sizzle of sensation, like his hand was waking up from being asleep.

"It means that it's going to hurt," said Jed.

Jericho's left hand twitched, the muscles fluttering in rapid fire movements.

"Jed, what's he doing awake?" asked another blond man, coming in. This one had the helix of medical snakes tattooed on his neck, which indicated that he was a doctor. Jericho realized that Jed only had one, which indicated that he was a field medic.

"Apparently, he's been treated with resistance therapies to Sonos-X," said Jed, without looking up from the display.

"Another brother?" asked Jericho as the doctor began to review the main panel display.

"Declan," said the doctor. "Cousin. Keelia didn't mention me?" Jed snorted.

"It's getting less funny," said Jericho and then winced as his hands flared into pain.

"Here's the deal," said Jed, sliding the display he was looking at around to Jericho. "You're here. You need to make it to here." He pointed to two spots on a graph—they looked extremely far apart with a few mountains of data in between them. "I've got some localized anesthetic I can give you, but I don't want to because that could impair your overall sensitivity later."

"So it's better if I just make it through?" asked Jericho, gritting his teeth as his right arm spasmed.

"Yes," said Declan. "Sorry."

"How long?"

Declan and Jed exchanged looks. "We think about five to seven minutes."

Jericho stared at them and thought about laughing. They were really worried about it.

"Can you make that?" asked Jed.

"Yes," said Jericho. "It will be fine."

And it was. It hurt like fire, but it wasn't nearly as bad as nanites, and he could watch the progress on the graph. Having a finite distance to travel made everything easier. When it was done, Declan poked at him, took some readings, and then wandered off.

The lights dimmed an extra level in the corridor and Jericho guessed that they were hitting the ship's night zone. He found that although he did feel fine, he was tired again. "So I'm going to live?" asked Jericho as Jed pushed a few more buttons on the bed scanner.

"Oh, probably. But if you do, it will be in spite of all your efforts to the contrary."

Jericho smiled, his eyes drifting closed. He was starting to like Keelia's family.

"Jericho?" asked Jed, looking down with him.

"Mm?" He raised his eyelids with an effort.

"Are you in love with my sister?"

Jericho stared at Jed. The medic didn't look particularly upset, but he did look serious. He probably deserved a serious answer.

"Yes," said Jericho.

Jed nodded and patted his arm before walking away. Jericho felt the pressure through the bandages and blankets, but he wasn't sure what it meant.

The next time he opened his eyes, it was still dark, but there was another man sitting in a chair next to the bed. He was sipping something that smelled suspiciously like real coffee and reading an actual paper book in the light from the scanner next to the bed. This man looked sort of familiar. Jericho's memories of the battle at the Nazari moon base were returning to him and he thought he'd seen this one in the crowd.

"Let me guess, you're Keelia's brother and you can't believe she didn't mention you?"

The man grinned and put his cup and book on the bed next to them. "Easton," he said standing up.

"How many of you are there?" asked Jericho.

"Just the six," said Easton. "Let's see, you've met Jed and Niall. Then there's me and Graves."

"Twins," said Jericho, the memory resurfacing.

"Yes," said Easton. "Then there's just Anwell and Mataxlen, who everyone just calls Mat."

"And cousin Declan?"

"Oh, lots of cousins," said Easton, smiling again. "Plus, Mom and Dad, and the aunts and uncles, and in-laws, and a few steps, and grands, and extras and plus ones."

"Keelia said *family*," said Jericho. "I didn't understand that there was so many of you."

Easton smiled again and perched on the edge of the bed. "She probably didn't think she needed to. We don't go too many places that don't understand the uh… breadth of the Black Swans."

"Huh," said Jericho. "It was just my dad and me. And Fang. But I stopped counting her about the time she started keeping me in a cell."

Easton smiled, but looked embarrassed. "Yeah, that's actually why I'm here."

"What?" Jericho didn't understand what Easton meant.

"Sorry," said Easton, reaching his hand out and putting it on Jericho's head. "But it took a lot to get her out of the Soul Sucker. We can't have someone unstable. And we figured it was better me than Mom."

Jericho reached up for Easton's hand, but found himself lost in a buzz of memories, as if Easton were flipping through his brain like the pages of a book.

"This is the first Nazari homestead," said Marid, hands on his hips, beaming at the tiny dilapidated house.

There was Fang. His father's body. The day he'd found Sadiki in the closet.

"The second year, the rains came. And your great-grandfather began to build sandbag walls as the river flooded." Marid walked around the house and Jericho followed, stomping extra hard in the puddles, throwing up mud and grass.

There was Bruges, twisted in the electrified net as Fang stood over him with the spear, laughing. Phaedra screaming as her shipmates were killed. Pavel being forced to kneel.

"The rain was going sideways, the wind carried off trees. The river got closer to the house. But still, your great-grandfather carried sandbag after sandbag and built walls."

There was Sadiki plunging the needle into Fang's neck and his body falling to the floor.

"For three days and nights, your great-grandfather carried sandbags and built walls as the water rose. His neighbors gave up. They evacuated. They left their land."

There was Keelia standing before the burning eye.

Jericho tried to turn away, and when he opened his eyes, he

was home, standing before the first Nazari homestead. His father, in his rubber boots, stood with his hands on his hips before the door, beaming at the sad little house. Jericho's younger self was stomping the puddles and only half-listening. It was the first time Jericho had ever seen his own memory from the outside. Easton stepped up beside him.

"Finish the story," said Easton. "I want to know why you come back here."

"Your great-grandfather stayed," said Marid. "In the end the water came within two feet of the door, but it didn't touch a single floorboard. The water never entered the house."

"Ah," said Easton. "I see. You're the man building walls against the river. You kept the water out."

Jericho didn't know what to say. "It was close," said Jericho.

He blinked again and he was back in the med-bay.

"But the water stayed out," said Easton patting his shoulder. "That's the important thing. Sometimes people can't stop the water and it drags them down. Or even if the house stays standing, it's damaged forever. Keeping the water out is a triumph."

"It doesn't feel like it," said Jericho.

"Keelia said that too," said Easton. "But you're both still standing. Take the win."

The med-bay slid open and a tangle of people fell through the door.

"Shhhhhh," said someone. "We'll wake Jericho."

"Pavel," said Jericho. "If I wasn't awake, I'd be awake now."

"Lights," said Easton and the med-bay lights flickered on. Pavel, Keelia, and Phaedra, a tentacle around each of their shoulders, were struggling to maintain their feet as Bruges tried to flop onto his back.

"What the hell happened?" demanded Jericho.

"Shhh," said Phaedra. "No, wait, we already did that."

"Are all of you drunk?" Jericho asked in disbelief.

"So drunk," said Easton, shaking his head as if trying to clear the fumes.

As they watched, the three humans managed to lift Bruges onto a bed in a wavering ballet of ineptitude. Keelia spun off and slammed into his bed.

"We may have gotten Bruges a little tipsy," she slurred, trying to fall over. Easton pushed her upright. "Thanks."

"You can't get Bruges drunk," said Jericho, trying to free his arm of the blankets. "That's impossible."

"Ohhhhhhhhhh," groaned Bruges.

"Turns out, it's possible," said Phaedra, climbing onto a bed. "You just need a lot of booze. Tara helped." She looked around as if expecting to see someone. "Where's Tara?"

"She went to find Niall," said Phaedra.

"We drank a lot," said Keelia, focusing on Jericho again.

"A lot," corroborated Pavel, trying to get on the bed next to Jericho. Easton scrambled to move his coffee and book.

"No, that one's mine," said Keelia, turning her head. "I always sleep across from Jericho." Jericho realized that he could feel the end of her braid against his hand. It felt silky.

"Right." Pavel nodded, recognizing the validity of the argument, and went to a bed further down. Easton looked amused.

"Easton, you said you wanted to talk to him, what the…"

Declan stared at the collection of prisoners now occupying the med-bay. "Keelia! What do you think you're doing?"

Keelia straightened to her full height. "Preparing for a hangover. What are you doing?"

"Kicking you out of the med-bay. Kicking you all out!"

"Good luck moving the Octoparian," said Pavel, pulling a blanket over himself.

Jericho laughed.

"Tell them to leave," demanded Declan, looking at Jericho. "Those ones are yours. Tell them to leave."

"They're drunk," said Jericho. "And I don't want them to. I'm taking the win."

"What?" Declan looked confused.

"That's right," said Keelia, and made an offensive arm gesture, which threw her off balance.

"Let them stay," said Easton, catching Keelia and pushing her up onto the empty bed. "There's really no point in moving them now. They'll just be back for help with their hangovers in the morning."

"They have perfectly good guest quarters," complained Declan.

"And they want to be here," said Easton reasonably. "Let it be."

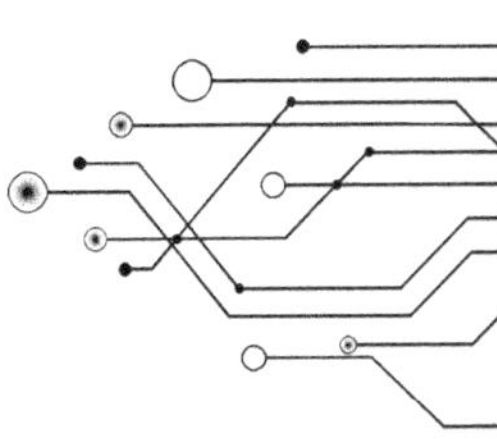

 Chapter 35

KEELIA & JERICHO

Keelia looked around the crowded dining room. Phaedra and Pavel looked to be having the time of their lives. Bruges was surrounded by half the science team, and from the flurry of signing, they were deep in conversation about the saline mating habits of… fungus? She wasn't sure she was reading that right. Keelia glanced up at Jericho—he had a slightly glazed look. She suspected that he found the sheer amount of interaction with other humans overwhelming. He'd spent the last two days with a steadily filling com bracelet of messages and roster of holo-meetings as his company and lawyers discovered that he was still alive. Getting time alone with him, even now that he'd been released from the med-bay, had been difficult. In the brief snippets of conversation that she'd been allowed, she'd learned that he had plans for everyone.

Bruges, when he had been snared by Fang, had been looking for new home waters for his family. Jericho's planet had an ocean and algae farms that he thought would be a good match and Octoparians were incredible sea farmers and researchers. The solution could not have been more obvious. Phaedra would be his head of security. Getting back through whatever wormhole that had brought her here was apparently not an option. Pavel wanted to visit his family, but he had promised to return. He and Jericho had some sort of plan for mining operations on the asteroid belt that had apparently been acquired in his absence. The only thing Keelia hadn't heard was what his plans were for her.

Which was ridiculous because, obviously, she had her own plans. She was going to be an engineer and help the family. She didn't need him to make plans.

She looked up at him again. Declan had said not to wear him out and Jericho looked like he was barely tracking the conversations around him.

"Are you getting tired?" she asked.

"Yes," he said. "But I'm fine as long as no one expects me to actually hold a conversation."

"Sorry," said Keelia, feeling guilty. "I wanted to keep it to just the immediate family, but I was sitting on an Ocotparian and two completely eligible partners and the cousins were starting to get pissed."

"Not everyone could make it to the pool?" he asked, chuckling slightly.

"Right," she said, putting her hand on his arm. Maybe now would be the opportunity to slip away. Her com bracelet burbled with an incoming message and Keelia let out a strangled squawk as she saw the sender.

"Uh, uh. I got it. I got it. What do I do?" Keelia clutched her com bracelet and looked up at Jericho in wide-eyed panic.

"Got what, dear?" asked Rayna, turning away from a conversation as she heard the anxiety in Keelia's voice.

"My results! From the Engineering Guild."

"Open it, idiot," said Anwell.

She looked up at Jericho. "You know you passed," he said.

There was a note in his voice, something soothing in the timbre and register that eased the butterflies in her stomach.

"Right, right. Opening it."

Her finger hovered over the receive button and Anwell sighed impatiently, then reached over her shoulder and pushed the display button on her wrist so they could all see the message. There was a fountain of hologram fireworks from her bracelet.

Congratulations! You have been licensed as an Engineer, Level A.

She could sense her brothers clustering behind her as she read through the fine print. Pavel, Phaedra, and Bruges gathered next to Jericho to read from the other side.

"Well done," burbled Bruges, waving his arms in pleasure.

"Yeah, yeah, you passed a bunch of hard stuff," said Mat. "Yay. We had no doubts. Scroll to the ranked results."

She did as he asked. Her name was listed first, followed by a string of others.

"First," said her father and she could hear the smugness in his voice.

Pavel let out a low whistle as he read through the list of student rankings. "That's a list of big family names that you're sitting on top of."

"No," said Jericho. "That's a list of people who can suck it."

"*Fjandinn* right," said Anwell approvingly as he high-fived Jericho.

Jericho blinked at the impact on his hand, surreptitiously rubbing his fingers afterward as if surprised by the sensation.

"Way to go, Keels," said Niall, picking her up and swinging

her around in a hug. The other hugs followed and Keelia found herself hugged and congratulated ruthlessly until she was finally returned, more or less, to her original position.

"First in your class. You're going to get a lot of job offers," said Rayna, smiling.

"Oh," said Keelia.

"Did you ever decide what you wanted to pursue?" her mother asked.

"Um, no. I kind of got kidnapped and held prisoner on a moon base."

"So you should have lots of time to decide," said her mother, her eyes twinkling. "Remember that you'll have to send all the offers to the Clan Council to be vetted for conflict of interest."

"Oh," said Jericho and she glanced up at him. His tone had sounded… surprised?

"And after you remember that," said her father, "you should also remember that the decision is entirely up to you."

She smiled at her father.

"Did you have something to add Mr. Nazari?" asked Rayna, reading the undercurrents of the room better than Langston, as usual.

"Um," said Jericho, looking nervously at Keelia, and then around the room at the assembled totality of Blacks. "I was going to talk about it with Keelia first, but I guess I'm here now."

"Yes," said Rayna, smiling a tad more wolfishly than Keelia thought appropriate. "You are."

"I have a lab. Or at least the company does. Fang used to run it. I was hoping Keelia would want to run it."

"I don't want to do weapons," said Keelia. Which wasn't at all what she wanted to say first, but it was the first thing that came out.

"No!" He took a quick step closer and then stopped, once again seeming to become aware that the eyes of her entire family were watching. "It doesn't have to be weapons—that was Fang. It was research and development. New products. Whatever is interesting. That's how Dad used to run it before Fang. The Nazari started as algae farmers and scientists—following in the footsteps of our Flaxenhart ancestors."

Keelia tried to turn the idea over in her mind. Her own lab. Doing whatever research she wanted. She'd certainly turned up a lot of interesting questions on the moon base. Questions that she hadn't had time to pursue. But what about Jericho? Was this a lab, or a lab and Jericho? Because she wanted both and one without the other might not be worth it.

"And where is this lab?" asked Rayna, ever the practical one.

"On my home planet," said Jericho. "We're going there now. I thought—" he turned back to Keelia. "I thought you could check it out. See if it was a fit." He sounded rather shyly hopeful and Keelia found herself smiling at him.

"I don't know," said Anwell. "If Keelia has a lab, you know Dad is going to be all over it. And won't that create intellectual property issues for anything Keelia develops for another company."

"What the hell would you know about intellectual property?" demanded Niall.

"Hardly a damn thing," said Anwell. "But I listen. I do know that it *is* a thing."

"No," protested Langston. "I could stay out of Keelia's lab." There was silence in the room as they all turned to look at Langston. Langston was almost universally adored among the Blacks. Keelia could see that no one wanted to outright say that he was a liar. "I think," continued Langston, looking guilty. "Maybe." He looked at Rayna.

"Of course, you could, dearest," said Rayna encouragingly.

"Actually," said Jericho, clearing his throat. "I thought of that. I thought maybe we could form some sort of joint venture and then he could have access to some parts, but not everything?"

"Ooh!" exclaimed Langston, looking excited. Keelia suppressed a chuckle.

Rayna looked thoughtful, as if weighing the likelihood of Jericho's proposal succeeding. "That sounds promising," she said. "But I have to say I'm not particularly excited about the prospect of leaving my husband or child in foreign territory."

"Oh, um." Jericho seemed to be processing that. "Well, there is a chunk of the planet coming up for sale. I was going to buy it, but I don't see why the Blacks or the Swan Clan couldn't own it. It would be your sovereign territory."

There was an inhalation of breaths around the room. Owning land was a Clan dream, but most habitable planets were locked down. And when pieces of planets came up for sale, the purchases were usually closed sales between first families. The only available planets were on the far reaches of explored space, far from any of the Black's business interests. Hardly ideal.

"What do you mean a *chunk* of the planet?" Keelia asked.

"I don't know. About a quarter, I think? My father left instructions to always buy land at home when it became available. This would be the last of it."

"The last of it?" asked Keelia, swallowing hard. "You mean, you own the rest of it?"

"Yes?" Jericho looked around the room as if looking for support.

"You said we were taking you to your planet. I didn't think you meant literally *your* planet," said Keelia.

"Well, obviously it's not *all* mine."

"Just three-quarters of it," said Keelia.

"Well, yes. My father liked to act like we pulled ourselves up by our bootstraps, but let's face it—great-granddad was a member of the first family of the TenDek Corporation and they practically built the Chimera Compact. Great-granddad financed the homestead and company with his corporate buy-out. Even for the fifth son of a fifth daughter, that was significant. Not that we haven't done all-right for ourselves since then."

"All right..." Keelia said, feeling slightly faint.

"But, Keelia," said Phaedra kindly. "He owned an entire moon base and asteroid."

"Hell, forget owning it," said Niall. "He could afford the fuel to fly it."

"But it was Fang's," protested Keelia.

"Yeah, 'cause nanites," said Pavel.

"You really didn't know he was ridiculously wealthy?" asked

Anwell skeptically. "Didn't you just spend six months in prison with him?"

"I had more important things to think about than Jericho's bank account! There were nanites and Fang and godsdamnned Soul Suckers and how to keep my feet warm!"

"You put on socks and shoes, Keels," said Anwell.

Keelia grabbed a drink from the table and began the swing to throw it at Anwell's head, but Jericho grabbed the glass and swung her around. He gulped the drink and made a thoughtful face as if surprised by the cocktail. "Socks and shoes were harder to acquire than you might think," he said to Anwell before turning to Rayna. "However, achieving some sort of agreement should not be."

"What does Keelia think?" asked Langston before Rayna could answer.

Keelia could feel the family looking at her. "I think," she said primly. "That I should like to go see this lab."

There was a cheer from the family and Rayna smiled. "The Council will still have to review it," she said.

"I'm willing to answer whatever questions they might have," said Jericho.

The family was having none of the formal nonsense and Keelia found herself being swept away for more congratulations and alcohol and dancing. When she finally escaped, she crept to the edge of the room and found Tara looking out at the stars from one of the viewing bubbles.

"That seemed to go well," Tara said as Keelia flopped down onto one of the chairs.

"Yes? I think. I just…"

"Just what?" asked Tara, sitting down next to her.

Keelia looked around. She didn't want to talk to her family about this—they were all too excited—but she did want to talk to someone.

"He didn't say anything about *us*," said Keelia, keeping her voice low.

"Ah," said Tara nodding. "It was all very businessy."

"Yes." Keelia glanced up at the older woman. She often felt out of her depth when it came to relationships. Somehow her mother never seemed to see that there were problems, and her brother's solutions were always useless.

"I wouldn't worry about it," said Tara. "You heard what he said. He'd intended to talk to you first, but your mom kind of forced his hand."

"Oh," said Keelia. "Yes, he did say that. And yes, she does do that. Why does she always do that?"

"Because she's looking out for everyone's best interests," said Tara. "But sometimes that's incredibly awkward, romantically speaking."

Keelia scrutinized Tara. "She had some sort of horrible chat with you, didn't she? I'm sorry. Was she awful? My parents are the worst."

Tara laughed. "At least she didn't do it in front of the entire family. No, it was fine. She just wanted to know my intentions toward her son and whether or not she should put me in the work duty roster."

"Oh," said Keelia, biting her tongue.

"And now you want to know what I said, don't you?"

"I really do," wailed Keelia. "But I don't want to pry."

Tara laughed. "I told her that I would be around until further notice. I'm kind of stuck on your brother."

"Well, I may be prejudiced, but I think he's worth being stuck on," said Keelia. "And you seem like you should have someone stuck to you."

Tara laughed again. "Well, hopefully Niall agrees with you. Meanwhile, you may wish to go retrieve Jericho. He looks like he may not be quite up to celebrating with all six of your brothers."

Keelia craned her head to find the knot of her brothers, who were talking over, around, and in front of Jericho. Jericho looked like he was fighting to stay awake. "Oh dear," said Keelia. "Declan really did say not to wear him out. They are not helping at all."

"No," agreed Tara. "They really don't even look like they're trying."

Keelia got up with a sigh, impulsively hugging Tara as she went. Tara looked surprised, but hugged her back.

"Niall," said Keelia, pulling at the knot of her brothers. Niall turned to look at her. "Niall, Mom had some sort of horrible talk with Tara."

"What?"

"I think everything's fine, but you should go tell Tara that she's gorgeous."

"Right," said Niall and disappeared into the crowd.

"Anwell," said Keelia, peeling off the next brother. "I think one of the cousins is trying to start a drunk game of hull hoops on C deck."

"Ah, yes!" Anwell began working his way through the crowd.

"Matty," said Keelia. "Do you know if they ever figured out the accelerator problem on the X-9?"

"Ah, crap. Where's Rufus? I meant to ask him about that."

"Jed," said Keelia. "Do you really think this is good for Jericho's health?"

Jed looked startled and glanced at Jericho, who was listening with apparent intentness to Graves and Easton. "Oh. No? Sorry. You should probably get him out of here."

They both turned to look at Easton and Graves. The twins looked up and then at Jericho. "Ah, right," said Easton. "Sorry." He patted Jericho on the shoulder and then they left with Jed.

Jericho looked around in surprise. "What just happened?"

"I got rid of my brothers," said Keelia.

"I didn't know that was possible," he said. "They seem like they're everywhere, or at least always around every time I try to talk to you."

Keelia grinned. "That is one of their specialties," she agreed. "Come on, we'll sneak out while no one is looking."

"Won't someone be upset?" He looked around.

"I doubt it," said Keelia, pulling him by the sleeve. Declan had said that he could get temporary sensory dampening with too much input and she'd noticed how careful he had been to not touch a lot of things all evening, so she didn't grab his hand.

Once on the promenade outside the ballroom, she slowed down to a stroll and tucked her hand into his arm.

"I know I was just complaining about them," he said. "But I do like your family."

"We're not too bad," she agreed and he laughed.

They reached the juncture where they had to choose a direction, and Keelia paused, feeling suddenly awkward. It was time to find out if Jericho's interest was with the family or with her.

"Which way?" he asked.

"So," she said, clearing her throat. "Left is the way to the guest quarters. But right is the way to my quarters."

"Right it is," he said, putting action to words.

They walked in silence and Keelia thought that probably ought to feel awkward too, but it didn't. She wondered if he found it odd that she talked now. Lots of things felt odd to her now that she was no longer under Fang's thumb. He'd been imprisoned even longer. She wondered what he found the most different. She took a breath to begin the question and he laughed.

"I used to love it when you did that," he said.

"Did what?" she asked blinking up at him.

"You would be so far away and then you'd come back with a question."

"Only then I couldn't ask it! It was so frustrating!"

"Yes, but I liked watching you remember I was there."

"I always remember that you're there," Keelia said, blushing. "I'm not a total spaz like Dad. I do remember who I'm talking to and to eat and dress myself." They arrived at her door and she opened it with her palm print.

"That seems like a remarkably low bar," said Jericho, his eyes twinkling.

"I like to make sure I can succeed," she replied.

He looked around her room and she felt nervous for the first time. She watched him take in the bedroom with the ratty, but so comfortable chairs, stacks of books, and double bed with the ridiculous mound of bedding that made her feel like she was sleeping in a nest. What if he thought it was weird? What if he realized *she* was weird?

"I love how much color is on this ship," he said, smiling at the blue painted walls. "You have my glaive," he said, pointing to his weapon that she'd carefully placed on a stand under the vid-screen.

"Yes," she blushed again. "It's traditional for, um, lovers to keep each other's weapons when one is injured."

"Well, what am I responsible for?" he asked, looking around. "Where are your weapons?"

"I don't have any. I'm not a fighter." He laughed out loud.

"What?" Keelia was confused.

"I think that's the first time you've ever lied to me. It was funny."

"I'm not lying. I'm not a fighter."

"So you didn't choke out Pavel?"

"Well, I have a basic understanding of self-defense. I am a Black, after all. But I don't know how to battle anyone or carry weapons or anything."

"Right," he said, nodding. "You don't battle people. Just Soul Suckers and nanites and insane despotic undead women and whatever else crosses your path."

He stepped closer and put his arms around her waist.

"That wasn't battling," objected Keelia as he kissed her. "That was engineering."

"Well, if you get sick or injured, I'll be sure to take care of your computer."

He pulled back, his hands burying themselves in her hair. He smiled as if enjoying the sensation. "How many times did I want to touch you?" he asked, quietly, his hands drifting from her face, to her neck, her shoulders, her body. "You were so close and I could never touch you." She didn't reply but put up her face to be kissed, and he complied.

"How many times did I try to say your name?" she said, when she could draw a breath.

"Say it now?" he suggested as his hand came to rest on her hip, pulling her into him as he kissed her neck.

"Jericho," she whispered into his ear, and his hand on her hip clenched. She worked his shirt up between kisses. It was strange to see him without the craze of nanite scarring.

They fell onto the bed and he laughed, batting back a comforter. "This all feels so strange," he said, as he ran a hand up her now nearly naked body.

"That's not what a girl likes to hear in this situation," said Keelia and he laughed again.

"You don't feel strange. *You* feel wonderful. What's strange is that I can feel everything. I hadn't realized how much I'd lost."

Keelia didn't know how to respond to that, so she kissed him. He pulled back after a moment and pushed her hair out of her face. "I meant that, you know. I didn't realize how much I had lost until I met you, and you have given me back everything I lost. I love you, Keelia Black."

"And I love you Jericho Nazari," she replied.

And after many adventures, the king and the queen, along with her six brothers lived many long years in happiness and peace.

Jacob and Wilhelm Grimm, The Six Swans

Dear Reader

Word-of-mouth is crucial for any author to succeed. If you enjoyed the book, please leave a review on your favorite book sales or review site. Even if it's just a sentence or two. It would make all the difference and would be very much appreciated. Search for: *Bethany Maines* on any book review site such as Goodreads, BookBub, Amazon and more.

Thank you!

Learn more about the Tesseract Box

and start the adventure at the beginning with

The Little Nebula from Karen Harris Tully

Take a sneak peak at Chapter One on the next page...

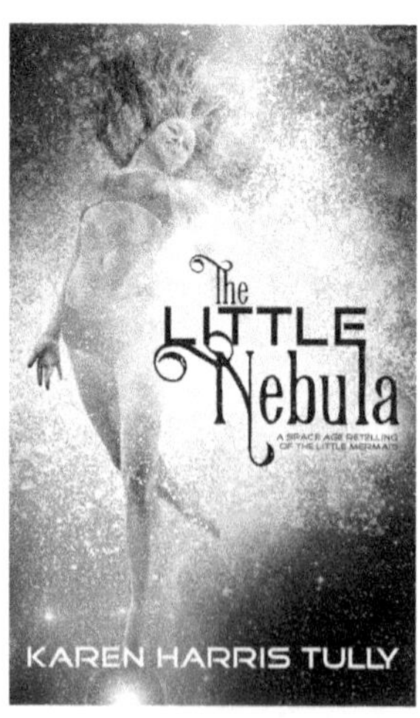

The Little Nebula

"[T]he youngest was the prettiest of them all; her skin was as clear and delicate as a rose-leaf, and her eyes as blue as the deepest sea; but, like all the others, she had no feet, and her body ended in a fish's tail."

Hans Christian Andersen, The Little Mermaid

Chapter 1:

SATELLITE SURFING

—Luminous—

Luminous was an energetic nebula, as far as nebulae go. Living in the cold, near-vacuum of space, made up of energy, gas, and dust, she refused to settle for the gravitational pull of any of the larger celestial bodies, like her siblings kept advising her. Why would she want that? Her surfing verged on art, creating beautiful aurora borealis above Earth. Plus, she loved to watch the fast-paced, short-lived people on its surface, both from above and through their holo-vision signals.

The humans were so full of life and noise, growth and emotion, as they floated through space on their blue-green planet. They were fascinating. They were also dirty, careless, and wasteful.

Look out below! Luminous crashed through a snarl of broken satellites and defunct space junk, surfing her once-favorite atmosphere: Earth's. The debris spiraled out of orbit in her wake to burn up on re-entry.

For many hundreds of Earth's orbits, the people had been extracting Earth's resources and turning it into trash. The space around the planet was now so full of human-made debris she could barely even surf her favorite spots. And now they'd turned to mining nearby asteroids to get more resources to create more short-lived junk for an ever-growing population. They could not seem to control themselves in creating either more garbage, or more people creating more garbage.

She'd tried talking to them, but communicating with humans was hard. She'd come to the conclusion that their attention spans were too short for meaningful conversation. Also, they didn't seem able to see her as anything other than random gas and dust. And so, she'd had to watch while they junked up the Earth's oceans, land, and her orbit. She'd had to devise a more direct way of communicating the problem to them.

Bombs away! she called in the universal language of radiation, though humans did not seem to recognize it in the least. Undeterred, she gathered up some junk in her gaseous dust cloud and released it toward a newly-launched satellite. Pieces ricocheted off its solar panels and it fired boosters to right its course. But she couldn't have that. For humans to take action, she had to hit them where it hurt: in their brand new technology.

She stretched herself out and tumbled the satellite into her gaseous tentacles, swung it around, aimed and released it to enter Earth's atmosphere, burning toward the giant island of trash stuck in the swirl of the ocean's currents. She followed it up with a whole swath of debris and felt a deep satisfaction in returning some of the humans' litter to them. She knew aiming at cities would garner more attention to her cause, but she drew the line at terrorism.

Recently, over the last two hundred orbits or so, humans had actually been trying to deal with their discarded resources on Earth's surface and oceans. Skeptically she'd watched them build something they called the Elevator. It was a moving platform that rose from one of the land masses in the northern hemisphere up into space to a well-fortified satellite tethered in geo-synchronous orbit. She'd heard the excited chatter on the radio waves when it began working, and ever since, over the course of many orbits, humans had used it to shuttle large, compact trash cubes from the Earth's land and oceans up into space. Weak ion pulses set them on a long trail to their fiery demise in the Sun. But humans hadn't yet addressed the junk they'd left adrift above Luminous's favorite planetary atmosphere.

It hurt to see the Earth this way. But without being able to talk with humans, satellite destruction was her best—her only— method of communication.

As for the overcrowding, humans seemed to be trying out

several solutions, none of which had even made a dent. They had placed surface domes on the moon and planet Mars, but hadn't yet seemed to figure out how to create an atmosphere like Earth's in either place. And, they had built an enormous space station currently out near Luminous's home planet Neptune, which used thrusters to keep itself in a strange, unnatural non-orbit. She supposed they must have a reason, but stars if she could figure out what it was. They called it the Tersa Tellus Space Port.

So many ships had puttered their way out to the silver, double-ring port, including recently, the three biggest space ships yet. Though she couldn't talk with the humans, she could hear their excitement and knew this was a big deal for them. She kept hearing one word: colonies.

And then, the excitement spiked, with a strong added emotion: fear. She heard a mass of radio waves projected all around the Earth and saw more frenzied activity than any human event she'd ever witnessed. She had no idea what was causing it, except she kept hearing the same word over and over, in every language: Pangaloid.

She had no idea what a Pangaloid was, and the signals from the satellites she hadn't destroyed had been no help. She needed to consult her sister and best friend Astri, who liked to stay close to Neptune, but first she turned to look out at the distant, prophetic stars. What she saw there made her stop in her orbit. Any thoughts about chucking another satellite back to its makers died a fiery death. Could she be reading that right? Now she really needed to talk with Astri.

A ship came to the space platform and she moved in to see if she could find out more about what could be causing this fervor on Earth. But as usual, the people aboard paid her no attention, launching and burning a highly inefficient, fiery tail from the rear end of the ship. She followed and stuck with them as they came up to what appeared to be max speed. For such a fast-lived species, even their fastest space travel was glacial. She checked their trajectory and was fairly certain they were headed toward Neptune and the space port.

She tried to signal to the people on the ship that she wanted to talk, to warn them, and finally got their attention with a series of energetic flashes that brought them to their windows. But all they did was stare at her for a while. They pointed, their energies showing awe and wonder at the nebula somehow stuck in the wake beside them, like that was even possible. But they didn't seem to understand anything she radiated at them. She tried again and again, but it was almost like they couldn't see more than a tiny range of the entire radiation spectrum with those round, frontal sensors attached to their bulbous heads. In frustration and as a last-ditch effort, she tried making shapes at them, imitating with her gaseous cloud the shape of their own ship. They'd have to recognize that, right? But though one or two watched her for a while, their attention was short. They soon wandered off, and Luminous had to admit defeat.

She sped ahead of them to talk it all over with Astri. Luminous found her lazing around in one of Neptune's rings, absorbing the minimal sunshine that made it out this far.

She watched as Astri ricocheted off a meteoroid and spun off in a new direction. Sometimes Luminous thought Astri had forgotten she was a nebula. Or, maybe she simply preferred being solid.

Lu! Are you finally giving up on the blue-green monster? Come to relax with me?

Earth is not a monster, Astri. It's exciting. You should really come with me next time, for the people watching if nothing else.

They blew up Callisto! Just a few cycles ago!

True, which I'm sure was an accident. Luminous had thought they'd finally gotten to the point in their evolution that they weren't going to destroy themselves. And then they'd blown up one of Jupiter's moons. It wasn't very reassuring. *You're the one who retaliated by chucking satellite parts down on areas of dense human activity.* She reminded Astri. *Don't you think you can let it go and move on?*

We've seen their ships, Lu. They open up their maws and pull us out of orbit and then, she whispered dramatically, *they eat us.*

Astri, you're an energy being. Get off your rock and avoid them!

Luminous, you're a nebula. If you want them to understand you, you've got to be solid with them. Send their satellites back to the inhabited areas that sent them in the first place, I say. Now, that's a message they would hear.

Oh, but they're not as bad as you think, Astri! I mean, yes, they're capable of destruction, but also love, and kindness, and creativity, and problem-solving. Remember when they were heating the planet so much it was killing them? They solved that.

Halfway, Astri conceded. *They may have stopped the Earth from warming further, but they never did slow the great storms, or their consumption of every Earth resource.*

But they took the first step. They're making progress! Except, Astri, there's something new going on right now, and I need your help to figure what it is.

Astri expelled an exasperated puff of gas and spun away from Luminous. *You need help alright. Here's some advice: Stop surfing Earth. Stop watching them! Stop trying to get those tiny humans to do the right thing. You work too hard and they're going to do what they want no matter how much you try because they can barely see past their own puny lifetimes. Earth is a lost cause, Lu, and you won't be radiant forever. Stay and have some fun with me. You can surf right here!*

But surfing Earth made her feel like she was experiencing something bigger than herself. There was nothing else like it. She wished she could make Astri understand.

Instead, she gestured at the stars with her shifting extremities.

Astri, look at the stars. What do you see? Her own change in perspective hadn't made any difference. Astri was silent for a long moment, observing the prophetic stars, twinkling in their usual soundless song through space.

War, said Astri at last. *War is coming. War and destruction.*

Another Earth ship passed by and she followed them, towing Astri along despite her protests, still not knowing how to engage humans in a way they would listen. She trailed them a short way to that giant, gleaming ring in space, Tersa Tellus. It was slowly spinning, usually with some ships docked around its shell and humans working and frolicking in space vehicles nearby. Every once in a while, blue and red laser blasts slashed through space, reducing rogue meteors and comets to dust before they could impact the port.

But it wasn't the light show that caught her attention. One

look at that silvery, spinning ring and all thoughts of trying to talk with the humans again stopped. It was now clear why there was all the excitement and fear on Earth. A very strange, unknown type of ship, white and softly glowing, was docked at the port.

Humans were getting their first official alien visitors. But, Luminous sensed something much bigger than one alien ship docked at port. There was an energy shift in the solar system. She felt its incoming waves. And, a few stretching hops away, she found the source.

The ship was merely the tip of the alien iceberg. An entire new *planet* was now parked outside the Kuiper Belt, orbiting the ninth and farthest planet from the Sun, enormous, dark Planet IX. No matter that planets did not travel, not that she'd ever heard of, but this one was here, now. And its radiation signature was the same as the alien ship at port.

Planet IX was the one planet that Luminous, Astri, and their nebula siblings stayed away from, for it housed an energy being like them, and also, not like them. This one was older, old as the solar system, old as the galaxy. This one they knew simply as Ix, and they studiously avoided his creepy, extremely elliptical orbit, which would soon cross into the Kuiper Belt and come the closest to Neptune it had been in thousands of solar orbits. Did these aliens, on their strange lush planet, know about Ix? About the energy beings who quietly, sparsely inhabited the galaxy? What was the reason for their visit—Ix or the humans?

The traveling planet wasn't large by any means, only about half the size of Earth, but for a planet to travel, and to stay warm in the far reaches of space where everything else was ice—how was that accomplished? Had the humans noticed? More importantly, how would they react?

This last question was vital, because of the humans' star weapons. The time was long past when they could only blow up their own planet. She had seen the weapon they'd launched at poor Callisto, and she'd watched them unload multiple identical weapons at their space port. She hadn't worried much about it at the time. Ice moons couldn't shoot back, but now, well, she supposed it all depended on how their first alien encounter was going.

She felt worry build in her greater than she'd ever felt before. She tried to calm herself. Energy beings had been here long before biologicals, and would be here long after, she reminded herself. Energy beings did not interfere with the short lives of humans. But this? She looked at the verdant Traveler planet, in a place where no such planet had any right to be, and back toward Earth. It was not even a speck in the distance, but she could picture the beautiful, blue-green planet clearly. Humans had made terrible choices with their home, but they and the Earth were hers. This solar system was her home. There had to be some way she could help humanity avoid war with these Travelers. If she could only talk with them.

She tried at the port's great silver ring, but the humans were in too much of a frenzy with the alien ship being there to pay attention to a nebula out the windows. So, she headed back toward Earth to find another ship, on its long, slow jog to the space port, and hopefully someone who would pay attention to her warnings. Astri, curious, tagged along and they soon found what they were looking for. A human ship had recently launched from the Earth Elevator platform, and an unusual one. This one was super shiny, slightly faster than usual, and it held only one person: a pleasantly symmetrical young man.

READ MORE IN THE LITTLE NEBULA FROM KAREN HARRIS TULLY

Galactic Dreams

Volume 1

Volume 2

About the Author

Bethany Maines, a native of Tacoma WA, is the author of action adventure and fantasy tales that focus on women who know when to apply lipstick and when to apply a foot to someone's hind end. When she's not traveling to exotic lands, or kicking some serious butt with her black belt in karate, she can be found chasing after her daughter, or glued to the computer working on her next novel.

Find out more at:
BethanyMaines.com

Other Works by Bethany Maines

www.ingramcontent.com/pod-product-compliance
Lightning Source LLC
Chambersburg PA
CBHW071513110726
47908CB00003B/824